Betty Before

Betty Before

ILYASAH SHABAZZ
····· WITH ·····
RENÉE WATSON

SCHOLASTIC INC.

ISBN 978-1-338-55134-1

12 11 10 9 8 7 6 5 4 3 2 1   19 20 21 22 23 24

Printed in the U.S.A.   23

First Scholastic printing, January 2019

Book designed by Aimee Fleck

A society is measured by the progress of its women. My father said, "When you educate a boy, you teach a community; when you educate a girl, you raise a nation." I dedicate this book to his beloved wife, my mother, Dr. Betty Shabazz, whose belief in the potential of every single girl inspired me to share her story with you.

—Ilyasah Shabazz

For Milt Adams and Geoffrey Brooks, my high school teachers, for instilling in me a love of history.

—Renée Watson

Pinehurst, Georgia
1934 - 1940

For who hath despised the day of small things?
—Zechariah 4:10, KJV

Prologue

I WAS JUST A BABY WHEN GRANDMA MATILDA took me away from my mother. Not quite one year old, with just a few words forming on my tongue, a few steps wobbling into a walk. I don't know this because I remember, I know this because my Aunt Fannie Mae told me so.

We lived in Pinehurst, Georgia—the kind of place you find when you're looking for someplace else. Where the sun shined all day long, and at night, crickets sang song after song. The story goes: Grandma Matilda came for a visit. When she picked me up and held me in her arms, taking a good look at me, like grandmas do, she found a bruise on my neck. She asked my mother, "What happened to this child?" and my mother said she didn't know.

Grandma Matilda suspected that someone must have done something terribly wrong to me, and so she took me away.

After that day, my mother moved to Detroit and I stayed in Pinehurst with my Aunt Fannie Mae, who took care of me like I was all hers. Like I was a gift she had always wanted. She would tell me this story over and over, that my mother was just a baby herself when she had me. "Betty," she'd say, "she was too young to know what to do with you." And I think this was my Aunt Fannie Mae's way of telling me that I should not go disliking my mother, not go blaming her for leaving me, because she didn't know how to raise a baby on her own.

But Aunt Fannie Mae knew what to do with me. I don't know how she got so good at loving. How she thought to tell me every day that I was her sweet brown sugar. How she knew just when to take my hand in the heart of her palm, holding me tight like she would never let me go. My Aunt Fannie Mae knew how to make a good day even better. And on bad days, she tried her best to make *me* feel better. Whenever I was afraid, she knew how to make me believe everything would be just fine. And any question I had, she took her time to answer. But there was one day when she couldn't comfort me, couldn't answer my questions.

It was the first time my Aunt Fannie Mae looked frightened.

It was the first time I saw a lynching.

We were on our way home from buying groceries at the market. Aunt Fannie Mae was telling me about the cobbler she was going to make. How she was going to mix the brown sugar, cinnamon, and butter with the fruit we'd bought, and then she just stopped talking. She snatched me up real fast with one hand and held me close to her heart. The apples and peaches fell from her left hand and rolled out of the bag. I looked at Aunt Fannie Mae's face and followed her eyes.

They were looking at one of the magnolia trees down the road. The tree had two bodies—a man's and a woman's—dangling from the branches like too-heavy Christmas ornaments.

"Close your eyes, baby," she said to me.

I don't know how long we stood there, but it was long enough for me to see fear in my Aunt Fannie Mae's eyes and feel that fear in my heart. My aunt was frozen and silent, and the only sound I could hear was her deep breathing. In, out. In, out.

But I couldn't look away.

I loved that tree. Just the day before, my friends and I had climbed it. We'd stretched our hands out as far as the tips of our fingers could go, touching the wind, trying to reach heaven. And now Negro bodies were swaying from it, side to side, side to side.

"Close your eyes, Betty," Aunt Fannie Mae said again. She put me down and we turned around. "We'll walk the long way home." She moved fast, pulling me along because my stride was shorter than hers and I could barely keep up. She squeezed my hand, never letting me go.

We left the fruit and the bodies behind. The whole way to our house, I wondered which would rot faster.

When we got home, we were quiet through supper, and when bedtime came, Aunt Fannie Mae kissed me and said, "Don't you ever forget how much Aunt Fannie loves you, Betty." But even with all of her love, I still had many questions.

I asked Aunt Fannie Mae, "Who killed that man and woman?"

She said she didn't know.

I asked Aunt Fannie Mae, "Why do Negro people die that way?"

She said she didn't know.

Aunt Fannie Mae must've known I had more questions that she couldn't answer, because that's when she told me, "Baby, some things we just have to take to the Lord. We have to pray for this world and ask God to help us. You know, God is always there to listen, baby. We can take all of our burdens and questions to Him. You hear me?"

So after each day settled into the black sky, my questions rose like the moon, hovering over me all night till I fell asleep. Most nights I asked the same questions over and over:

What did I do to make my momma leave me?

What can I do to make her love me?

I lived with my Aunt Fannie Mae until I was six. And when I turned seven, that's when my Aunt Fannie Mae died.

In just one day, I learned how love can disappear in an instant, like how if you blink you can miss the setting sun. In one day, my Aunt Fannie Mae went to heaven and I moved to Detroit.

Detroit, Michigan

1945

You can't sing about love unless you know about it.
—Billy Eckstine

One

"BETTY? BETTY…"

I hear my sister calling my name.

"B*eeee*tty . . ." Juanita's whisper floats across the room.
She shares a bed with Jimmie, I share a bed with Shirley.
When we were little, I didn't mind sharing a room with my
three younger sisters. Our small bodies didn't take up
much space.

But now, I am eleven.

And most nights Shirley's knees end up in my ribs.
Her arms stretch across my neck. The covers mostly just
cover her. And it's not sharing a bed that's so bad. It's
how Juanita wakes up in the middle of the night—*every*

night—needing to use the bathroom but too afraid to go into the hallway by herself. Even though we have a night-light in our room and one in the hallway.

"Betty, will you go with me?" Juanita is whining now, and her voice is getting louder.

I don't want her to go alone or to wake up Shirley and Jimmie, so I slide out of bed. "Come on," I whisper, holding out my hand in the dark. Juanita takes it and we tiptoe to the bathroom. I wait for her outside the door, leaning my sleepy body against the wall.

There's a family photo next to me that I can barely see in the darkness, but I know it by heart because it's been hanging there since I moved here four years ago. I am not in it. It's the first thing I noticed when Ollie Mae brought me home from the train station and took me to my bed-room. Which is when I found out Ollie Mae was not just *my* mother but also the mother of three other girls—Shirley, Jimmie, and little Juanita. And she was not just a mother, she was also a wife to Arthur Burke, who had two sons of his own. One was named Henry and the other Arthur, who everybody called Sonny. So in one day, I went from having one aunt, one grandma, and a bunch of baby dolls to having a mother, a father, three baby sisters, and two younger brothers.

Every time I see this photo, I think I really don't belong here. That my mother's house doesn't feel like home. And here's why: because Shirley, Jimmie, and little Juanita call our mother Momma and I call her Ollie Mae. Because Shirley, Jimmie, and little Juanita look like me but not fully like my sisters, since I am the one with a different daddy. I spent the first day staring at all of them when they weren't looking—especially Ollie Mae—trying to find myself in the arch of her eyebrows, the shape of her nose. I studied the thickness of her hair, her thin frame.

And her eyes. They looked sad all the time, even when she was smiling. Her eyes were always apologizing, like she was telling me she loved me but in a different kind of way. Like how you love a mistake that ends up not being so bad after all. Like how you love the rain because even though it can make a mess of things, it still makes rainbows rise and flowers grow.

Juanita comes out of the bathroom yawning a thank-you,

and it only takes her a few seconds to fall back asleep once she's in her bed.

I'm wide awake now, lying on my back, looking at the ceiling. This is when all of the memories come flooding in. During the day, I'm too busy with schoolwork or housework or going to church or fussing at Sonny and Henry for the way they tease Shirley and hide Jimmie's dollies, or how they jump out from behind the sofa and scare little Juanita. But at night, after I take Juanita to the bathroom and we return to our bedroom, she falls fast asleep and I am the one tossing and turning, tossing and turning. I am trying to hold on to the sound of my Aunt Fannie Mae's laughter and the taste of the fruit cobbler and butter pecan ice cream we'd make from scratch, how I'd sit on the floor between my Aunt Fannie Mae's knees getting my scalp oiled, my hair braided in two long plaits with pretty ribbons on each side.

I close my eyes and replay these memories over and over every night. But not only the good memories have stayed. Sometimes, when I'm not even trying to remember, I see those magnolia trees, the blooming white flowers, and the thick brown branches with Negro bodies hanging.

A tree can never be just a tree after seeing that.

I lie on my back, then my stomach, then my side. I kick my leg out from under the covers, pull them back over me, take them off again.

I fall asleep talking to God:

Is my Aunt Fannie Mae there with you, Lord, looking down on me, watching everything that's going on?

Does my Aunt Fannie Mae know how much I miss her? How much I love her?

Will Ollie Mae ever look at me the way she looks at my sisters?

I toss and turn, turn and toss, and think about that photograph in the hallway, then back to my Aunt Fannie Mae, then I think of those haunted trees again. I think that maybe all of these memories are another reason I still feel like a stranger here. Even though I am far away from Pinehurst, I've brought the South with me.

❦

Sunday's sunlight fills our room the next morning. I feel like I just closed my eyes, and already it is time to wake up and get ready for church. Every single Sunday we go to

Bethel African Methodist Episcopal Church. First, everyone goes to Sunday school. We split up by age—the adult class, the high school class, the middle school class, and then there's a class for the younger kids, and a nursery for the babies. We learn stories from the Bible and lessons on how to be better people. Besides the time when the choir sings, Sunday school is my favorite part about church. I look forward to it every Sunday.

Ollie Mae is standing at the bedroom door. She doesn't know I'm awake, doesn't know that I know she does this every single morning—that she opens the door and just stands there and stares at me before she wakes us. Maybe her mind is like my mind. Maybe it jumps from one memory to the next, bouncing like a rubber ball. I wonder what memories she keeps of Pinehurst.

Sometimes I ask Ollie Mae about her memories, but she usually just changes the subject or gives me one-word answers like she doesn't remember anything.

Ollie Mae stands there for a minute more, sighs, and says, "Okay, girls. Rise and shine. You, too, Betty Dean."

I fake a yawn, stretch my arms, and slide out of bed.

Jimmie never eases into a morning. She takes charge in

everything she does. Jimmie leaps out of bed, singing, "Good morning, Momma."

But Ollie Mae is already out of sight.

We move about, making our beds the way Ollie Mae likes them, and take turns going in and out of the bathroom, bumping into and stepping over one another. I help little Juanita get dressed because even though she can do it herself, she takes too long. "Lift your arms," I tell her. She lifts them and wiggles into her blue-and-white polka-dot dress.

Shirley slips her feet into her black Mary Janes and buckles each shoe. Then she looks in the mirror and turns right to left, smiling at herself. Knowing Shirley, she might change before we leave. She is always checking and re-checking herself in the mirror, making sure she looks just right. Shirley turns to me and says, "Betty, I had a dream last night, but I can't remember what happened."

"If you can't remember it, then how do you know you had a dream?" Jimmie asks. She sees me brushing my hair, so she brushes hers, too.

"I just know. *And* it was funny." Shirley can tell she's not making any sense.

I laugh and then Jimmie laughs, even though I'm not sure she understands what's funny. Jimmie is just a few years younger than Shirley. Whatever I do, Jimmie does. She's my little chocolate drop.

Ollie Mae calls to us from the kitchen. "There's a lot of giggling and talking going on up there," she says. "Better be some getting ready up there, too. Breakfast is on the table."

Sonny and Henry speed down the stairs, and we are right behind them.

Shirley keeps talking her silly talk. "But doesn't that happen to you, Betty?" she asks me. "Don't you sometimes wake up feeling like you had a dream about something but the details are gone?"

"Sometimes," I tell her, just to make her feel like she's not the only one. Shirley, Jimmie, and little Juanita trail behind me like ducklings, watching my every move and listening to my every word. "But sometimes? Sometimes, you remember every detail. Sometimes they are so real that if you were laughing in your dream, you wake up laughing. And if you were crying, you wake up crying."

"Oh. That's never, ever happened to me," Shirley says.

"Me, neither," Jimmie echoes. She sits down in her chair, barely able to keep still. She reaches for the biscuits in the middle of the table, then pulls her hand back quick when Ollie Mae says, "We haven't prayed yet."

"Yes, ma'am," Jimmie says.

Arthur clears his throat. "Let's bless the food. We can't be late for Sunday school." Arthur prays—too long for someone who just said he was worried about being late.

We can barely get our amens out before Shirley says, "Momma, I had a funny dream last night, but I can't remember it. Does that ever happen to you?"

Shirley's talking so much she's barely eating, and I'm thinking how cold her eggs, bacon, and cheesy grits are going to be. I'm thinking how different we are that she can't keep her thoughts in her head, while mine won't go away.

Ollie Mae tells her to finish her breakfast and focus on one thing at a time. Shirley finally stops talking about her dream and says, "I've got to practice my Sunday school verse." She sits up straight, closes her eyes, and starts reciting Philippians 4:13. "I can do all things through Christ which strengtheneth me. I can do all things through Christ which strengtheneth me. I can do all things through Christ which strengtheneth me." She takes a breath and then tells us, "If I say it right at Sunday school, I get a gold star on the chart, and everyone who gets ten gold stars by spring can go to Belle Isle Park!"

"Really? I want to go!" Jimmie says. "And it's an island, not a park." She chomps on her bacon.

Shirley drinks her milk, and in between sips she's still talking. "You have to memorize ten Bible verses plus the books of the Old and New Testaments. And it's a park."

Jimmie's shoulders shrink.

Arthur looks at Shirley. "Watch your manners. And be nice to your sister," he says.

"It's both," I tell them. "An island that's a park." I eat the last of my eggs.

"Who cares?" Sonny shouts. And for that he gets a stern look from Arthur, so he mumbles, "Sorry."

Shirley just keeps on talking. "We're going to swim, paddle canoes, and go to the aquarium to see all the beautifully colored fish. And then we'll have a picnic lunch."

"I want to go!" Jimmie pouts and looks at Ollie Mae.

Arthur says, "Well, you better get to studying the scriptures. That's the only way you can join them." Then Arthur and Ollie Mae get up from the table. "All right, it's time to go," Arthur says.

Jimmie brings her plate to me. I wash it and put it to the side of the sink with the others so I can dry them and place them back in the cupboard before we leave.

"Get your coats and your gloves, too," Ollie Mae tells us. "This November air is brisk."

I put the last plate away in the cupboard, put my coins in my pocketbook for the offering, grab my coat and my Bible, and close the door behind us.

Jimmie grabs my hand as we walk to church. Ollie Mae trails behind to walk beside me. She says real low, "Betty Dean, I want you to behave yourself today in church, you hear me? Don't think I didn't see you and your friends passing notes during service last week." Ollie Mae looks at me.

"Yes, ma'am," I say.

Two

ONCE SUNDAY SCHOOL IS OVER, THE FIRST thing Shirley tells me is that she got the gold star. "Nine more to go," she says.

"That's great, Shirley!" I say.

We join the other kids who are rushing over to Mrs. Malloy, making sure we smile real big. She gives each of us a piece of candy every Sunday as long as we promise to wait till after church to eat it. Mrs. Malloy is married to one of the head deacons, and she's also one of the organizers of the Housewives' League with Mrs. Peck. Mrs. Peck is Pastor Peck's widow. She started the Housewives' League to help support Negro businesses. She organizes the boycotts of stores that refuse to hire Negroes or sell products made by Negroes. They say since the store owners don't want to hire us or sell our products in their stores, we shouldn't spend our money there. Lots of folk around here call Mrs. Malloy and Mrs. Peck Detroit royalty.

I see what they mean. Mrs. Malloy's fingernails are always polished so perfectly, like the shiny pearls she wears around her neck. And her shoes! Mrs. Malloy's husband owns a shoe repair store, so her shiny patent leathers always look brand-new. Each Sunday she wears a different hat, sometimes one with netted lace hanging over her eyes, sometimes one with a big, wide brim. Her suits always match her hats. Plus, she smells really nice, like flowers. She is tall and slender, with just a few wrinkles in her face and not one in her clothes.

Mrs. Malloy greets me the same way every Sunday: with the biggest smile that wakes up something deep inside me. "Good morning, Betty," she says as she gives me a hug. "Baby, do you know how beautiful you are?"

I smile and nod, thinking, *Yes I do, because my Aunt Fannie Mae told me so.* Hearing Mrs. Malloy say it, too, makes me believe it just a little more because she is not my aunt, or my grandma, or a family member at all, so she doesn't have to say sweet things to me.

Mrs. Malloy doesn't have any children, but still, she knows how to love, how to look at you in a crowd like you're the only person she sees.

I take my piece of candy and walk over to my best friends, Suesetta and Phyllis, who are sitting in the sixth row, right side. We go to the same school, too, so we pretty much see each other every day except Saturday. I sit at the end of the pew, next to Suesetta, who is wearing a navy-blue skirt, a white starched shirt, saddle oxfords, and bobby socks. Her hair is pressed and curled real tight at the ends. Phyllis's hair is pulled back into a ponytail. Phyllis is the wiry one. Her long, thin arms and legs don't have much body to hold on to. She has light-brown skin, like Suesetta.

Ollie Mae walks right over to us, says, "Betty Dean, I've got my eyes on you. You follow the rules in the Lord's house. You hear me?"

"Yes, ma'am," I say.

Pastor Dames takes the podium. He's only been the pastor for about a year. He came to lead our church after Pastor Peck died. It's so different without Pastor Peck being here. I didn't think anyone could ever replace him. It's different not seeing him at the pulpit or after church greeting the visitors with Mrs. Peck, who still comes to church and sits in the same pew every Sunday. Somehow she is still able to smile and praise God even though her husband is gone.

The service starts off with a prayer and the reading of scripture. Then comes my favorite part: the choir. They sound like heaven's angels. I am nodding my head and tapping my feet to the rhythm and singing along. Suesetta turns to me, whispers, "You should join the youth choir, you have a nice voice."

"Thank you," I say. I continue to sing, praising the Lord.

I slide my hand in my purse and pull out the peppermint Mrs. Malloy gave me. I make sure no one is watching—especially Ollie Mae—then unwrap the candy and put it in my mouth fast, holding my hand up to my face and faking a cough.

Suesetta pokes me in the side with her elbow. "I want one," she whispers.

"I don't have any more."

"Well, let's go to the candy store and get some," Suesetta says.

"Okay. I'll ask Ollie Mae if I can walk with you after church."

One of the women in front of us turns around and gives us the eye that tells us to stop talking.

We lower our whispers.

"Not after church," Phyllis says. "During offering time."

The woman turns around again, this time clearing her throat.

I don't respond. I just keep looking straight ahead at the choir, start clapping my hands. There's no way I can skip out on church to get candy. The last time Suesetta and I followed along with one of Phyllis's it-won't-take-long adventures was when we stopped by the ice cream parlor after school instead of going straight home. I made it to my house just before Ollie Mae did, so she had no idea, but I could barely enjoy my ice cream because the whole time I was worrying about getting a whipping. My stomach twists like a licorice just thinking about it. Besides, I know Ollie Mae has her eyes on me. Today is not the day to go to the candy store.

Once it's offering time, the deacons stand at the front of the church asking the congregation to rise and follow the ushers from the rear.

Phyllis whispers, "Keep some of your money for the candy store." Then she says, "Walk out of the sanctuary like you're going downstairs to the restroom."

When she says this, I feel like that's a much better plan than just leaving. If Ollie Mae sees us walk out of the sanctuary, she'll think we went downstairs to the restroom or maybe to get a drink from the water fountain. We walk a long circle around the sanctuary and when I get to the front, I place one nickel in the basket instead of two. I walk past Deacon Malloy, who is holding the basket, and I smile.

Suesetta and Phyllis are right behind me and I can hear Phyllis saying, "Just keep walking . . . Keep . . . walking."

I know what I'm about to do is wrong. But sometimes I get tired of being the one who always listens and follows all the rules, the one who watches over Shirley, Jimmie, and Juanita.

I try to look normal, like the words coming out of Phyllis's mouth are just the lyrics to the song the congregation is singing.

Love lifted me, love lifted me. When nothing else could help, love lifted me.

With my nickel in my hand, I walk right past the pew where we were sitting and keep going, right out the door, down the block, around the corner to the candy store.

Suesetta and Phyllis follow me.

My heart is jumping and flipping and my hands are trembling. I don't settle down until I know for sure that no one is following us. "I can't believe we just . . . left," I say.

Suesetta looks at Phyllis. "How are we going to get back in without anyone seeing us?"

Phyllis laughs. "Do you know how long Deacon Malloy prays? If we hurry and choose what we want, we'll be back before anyone notices."

Suesetta looks leery of Phyllis's confidence, but we walk into the candy shop and start picking our candy. The man behind the register looks us over. He is dressed in black slacks, a white shirt, and a red bow tie. "Mighty dressed up just to come to a candy store, young ladies," he says. He gives us a disappointed look like adults do so well when you are not doing what they think you should be doing. I look away.

I get to thinking that maybe this was a bad idea, but it's too late. We're here, so I might as well get something, and quick. On the front counter there are two oversized jars full of gumballs, jawbreakers, and malted milk balls. The jars are sitting on top of a glass case displaying small pastries. I want a little bit of everything but I know that's impossible, so I rush past the jars and go to the aisles that have small boxes of candy.

Phyllis is there already, choosing what she wants. She picks up three pieces of bubble gum and one small box of Dots.

"You can't get those," I tell her. "Not if you're going to eat them in church."

"Why not?" she asks.

"We have to get something we can hide in our mouths. Not something we have to chew. Everybody will see us chewing bubble gum."

Phyllis says, "Good point." She grabs a pack of sour suckers. "We can share these."

I pick up three candy drops. "And these, too. But after church so it won't matter if our tongues change colors."

Suesetta gets three Sugar Daddies. "For after church," she says.

I pay five cents for my candy, Suesetta and Phyllis pay for theirs, and we leave.

29

On the way back to church, Phyllis hands out equal amounts of sour suckers to each of us. The rest of the candy is in my pocketbook.

We stop in the foyer and, instead of entering the sanctuary, we go straight downstairs to the basement and take our turns coming out of the bathroom just in case someone asks where we were. Now, we won't be fibbing if we say the bathroom. We sneak back into the sanctuary like we never really left. Step right back into our row, candy in our cheeks, just as Pastor Dames begins his sermon.

He asks the church to stand for the reading of scripture and says, "Turn your Bible to Galatians 6:7." We flip the pages and follow along as Pastor Dames reads out loud. "Be not deceived; God is not mocked: for whatsoever a man soweth, that shall he also reap." Pastor Dames closes his Bible. "Church," he says, "when you sow injustice, you reap calamity. When you sow hatred and selfishness, racism and fear, you reap destruction and chaos!"

The church mothers nod, fanning themselves with the church bulletin. A few people stand, clapping and saying, "Yes, Lord. Yes!"

Pastor Dames says, "Oh, my friends, the Lord will not allow this suffering to last forever. The Lord's timing is not your timing. We must not be weary. For every tear you sow, you will reap joy. For every good deed you've done, kindness and provision and peace will be at your doorstep."

More people stand, more hands get to clapping.

He pauses and speaks real slowly, "I have been young and now I am old. We have come a long way as a people." He looks around the congregation as his voice gets loud. "As slaves, we cultivated this nation's barren land and we turned it into a land of milk and honey so that every single American citizen now has the opportunity to call this great United States of America his home," he preaches. "Our people did that. Your people did that, Church. The time for suffering will soon end." The whole congregation is standing now, clapping and cheering. The pastor shouts, "The fight for freedom and equality for all of our children must continue until every single American is free. Until there is truth and justice for all of God's children."

Pastor Dames is quiet for a moment, letting his words

sink in, letting the amens and hallelujahs echo throughout the sanctuary. "Church, we must not fight hate with hate. We must continue to sow goodness, forgiveness, love. We serve a mighty God. And He will take care of us. He always does." Pastor Dames wipes his brow with a white handkerchief. He takes a sip of water, then lowers his voice, talking solemn and low. "And this goes for our personal lives, too. Let us remember that God sees everything. He sees our heart, every good deed, and every sin. Every word of gossip, every lie. God sees and hears it all."

I swallow my candy, look down at the floor, my shoes, anything but Pastor Dames's eyes. Did he see us leave church? Does he know I spent some of my offering money on candy?

Pastor Dames ends his sermon with a prayer, asking God to give us all the strength to continue to do good even in the face of pain and injustice. And then, he says, "And Father, forgive us for the times when we fall short and don't do what we should."

"Amen!" I say. Real loud.

Three

AFTER CHURCH SUESETTA SAYS, "PHYLLIS IS coming over to my house. We're going to listen to her Billy Eckstine record and bake cookies. You want to come?"

"I'll be right back," I tell them, and run to find Ollie Mae to ask permission.

Ollie Mae says, "Do you think you deserve to go, Betty Dean?"

My heart tumbles to the pit of my stomach. Does she know I left church to get candy?

I stand there thinking about what I should say. I do not want to fib, especially in church. Especially because the last time I told a really, really tiny lie about eating all of my vegetables when really I gave them to Jimmie, Ollie Mae gave me a whipping. So I don't fib right here, right now in church. Because I don't know what Ollie Mae or the Lord might do. And I don't want her or the Lord upset with me. I think about what Pastor Dames said about reaping what we sow and so I pray one more time inside my head, asking God, *Please don't punish me for misbehaving.*

Ollie Mae sighs and says, "Well, answer me for God's sake. Do you think you deserve to go?"

I don't say anything. I just keep praying.

Ollie Mae steps to me and grabs my wrist, real tight.

She bends down low enough to whisper in my ear. "I let you sit with those girls today, Betty Dean, and you disobeyed me."

Mrs. Malloy sees us. She walks over, slow and calm, and stands close enough so Ollie Mae can see her but not so close that she's in our space.

Ollie Mae squeezes my wrist tighter. Her whisper is not light or sweet like the kind of whisper that tickles your ear. Hers is bitter and stinging. "I brought you into this world, Betty Dean, and I can take you out. You hear me?"

"Yes, Ollie Mae. Yes, ma'am."

Mrs. Malloy steps closer. "Everything okay?" she asks. But something in her voice tells me she knows nothing is okay.

Ollie Mae lets go of my wrist. "Everything's fine," she says.

"I'm taking Phyllis to Suesetta's house. Is Betty coming?" Mrs. Malloy asks. Suesetta lives next door to Mrs. Malloy, so she gets a ride to church every Sunday. Mrs. Malloy steps a little closer to Ollie Mae and says, "Betty really ought to spend some time with girls her own age, don't you think?" It doesn't sound like a question. "I'll have her back right after supper. I know tonight is a school night." Mrs. Malloy hardly gives Ollie Mae a chance to answer.

Ollie Mae looks at me, giving me another warning with her eyes. "You can go. I'll wait up for you," she says.

Suesetta, Phyllis, and I follow Mrs. Malloy to her car. We sit in the back seat and wait for the Malloys to get in. Mr. Malloy is talking with Deacon Boyd, Phyllis's dad, about everything and nothing—from the weather to sports to today's sermon. Mrs. Malloy is talking with Mrs. Boyd, and it seems like they might go on talking forever.

Deacon Boyd looks at Mr. Malloy's car and says, "I'm going to get me one of these automobiles now that General Motors is making Fords again."

"Yes sir, it will be good to get the factories back to making cars, instead of a car factory being used to aid the war. How many wars do we need anyway?"

Then Mrs. Malloy says to her husband, "Dear, we should get going," and the four of them say goodbye.

On our way to Suesetta's house, all I can think about is the candy that's in my purse and the whipping I'll get when I go home. I think about all the other ways Ollie Mae could punish me—no playing outside, extra chores, or a discussion about how what I did was wrong.

I think about all the things she'll say as she's whipping me, how she'll make me feel guilty, telling me, *After all I do for you*, and *You ought to be ashamed of yourself*, and *If you're going to live in my house, you are going to live by my rules.*

And then I think, *What if I stop living there?*

Maybe I can stay with Suesetta.

Maybe Phyllis.

Maybe I can go back to Pinehurst. Maybe a friend of my Aunt Fannie Mae will remember me. Maybe a long-lost relative will be found and want to take me in.

Suesetta takes me away from my thoughts. "Mrs. Malloy, Betty's going to join the youth choir. Did you know she can sing?"

"Well, no, I didn't," Mrs. Malloy says. "I bet there's all kinds of hidden talent in Betty that I don't know about." She smiles at me and I try to smile back, but my stomach is in knots thinking about Ollie Mae.

I start feeling better once we're at Suesetta's house. Her living room is huge, decorated with white-and-gold velvet drapes, blue-and-gold sofas, and thick royal-blue rugs that are under our feet. Chandeliers glisten above us. Every time I come over to Suesetta's I think about how much bigger her room is than mine and how it is all hers. She has a pink quilt covering her bed, with pink pillows. Across from the bed is a big wooden dresser with a matching mirror. She has lots of framed photos and colorful keepsakes. There's a photograph of her as a baby in her mother's lap. She is caught in a laugh and seems so happy.

I look away.

Besides her bed and a chair at her desk, there's a small sofa big enough to fit two people on it. I sit on the sofa, Phyllis sits on the chair at the desk.

There are suitcases leaning against the wall. Phyllis hands the record to Suesetta and asks, "Whose suitcases are those?"

Suesetta plays the record and Billy Eckstine croons his blues away. "My Uncle Clyde and Auntie Nina are staying with us for a while. My cousins Kay, Bernice, and their baby brother, Allen, too."

"They're all living *here*?" I ask. "But I thought they lived in Black Bottom." I remember meeting Uncle Clyde, Aunt Nina, and their children when they first moved to Detroit from Alabama, but I don't see them much. Uncle Clyde came to work at one of the Ford car factories, on the assembly line where they made parts for the machines the army used in the war.

Suesetta tells us, "My mom said now that all the soldiers are coming home from the war, they will need their jobs back and the factories will start making cars again, so

Uncle Clyde got let go. My mom said they'll be with us for just a little while. Until they get back on their feet."

"Where does everyone sleep?" Phyllis asks.

"Kay—the one who's sixteen—she sleeps in here with me. Bernice is seven and she sleeps in the basement with Uncle Clyde and Auntie Nina. The baby is only a few months old, so he sleeps with them, too."

Phyllis asks, "They have the whole basement to themselves?"

"Yup!" Suesetta says, and sits on her bed, which isn't made up. I think about how Ollie Mae would never, ever let me leave the house, let alone have company over, if my bed wasn't made.

"Are they ever going to move back to Alabama?" I ask.

Phyllis looks at me like I should know better than to ask a question like that. "There's nothing in the South to go back to, Betty," she says.

I want to say there's plenty to go back to. That my Aunt Fannie Mae's grave is there, and the house she raised me in, and my friends who lived down the road. My Grandma Matilda is there on her pecan farm. But I don't say anything because I also know there are good reasons why people who look like us would never, ever want to go back.

Billy's voice isn't singing anymore. Only the sound of his orchestra is filling the room.

Suesetta leaps off the bed and grabs me by both hands, pulling me toward her. "Let's dance," she says. The three of us strut our stuff, bebopping all over Suesetta's bedroom.

Suesetta and Phyllis are trying to move like me, but they can't. So Suesetta does her own thing and Phyllis plops down on the sofa.

"You think it's okay with God that we're listening to jazz and we just came out of church?" Suesetta asks.

My body is still moving and shaking, bebopping and gliding across the floor. Phyllis changes the record to Cab Calloway. "All those preachers at church say God made everything, right? Doesn't that mean music, too?" I say.

"I guess you're right," Suesetta says.

We dance a little while longer, until Suesetta switches the record again, puts on something slow. She returns to her bed and leans back on a pillow. I look in the mirror, check to see if my hair is messed up from all this dancing.

It still looks good. I read one of the posters hanging on the wall. I've never noticed it before, so it must be something new. The sign says, DON'T BUY WHERE YOU CAN'T BE HIRED. "Is that from the Housewives' League?" I ask.

"Yeah. Mrs. Malloy came by to talk with my mother about it. She said that Negroes should only buy from other Negroes. And if people don't like us because we're Negroes, we shouldn't give them our money," Suesetta tells us. "Did you know you could join as a junior member?"

"No. What does that mean? What do junior members do?" I ask.

"I think they go canvassing and also help set up for the teas and fund-raising banquets that the League puts on," Suesetta says. "And there are classes to take—well, not like the classes we have in school, but more like history classes about *our* history."

"We should join," I say.

All of a sudden Phyllis's face twists into a frown.

I sit down on the rug, leaning my back against the dresser. "Don't you think it would be fun to dress up and go to those banquets?"

Suesetta says, "That part sounds fun. I don't know about walking door-to-door to hand out flyers. Especially in the cold."

Phyllis is quiet. I look at her and before I can ask her if she wants to join, she says, "I'm not joining the House-wives' League, Betty. That doesn't sound like fun to me at all. Besides, my mom won't let me."

I can tell by the tone of her voice that she doesn't want to talk about it. She changes the subject real quick, not giving me a chance to ask any more questions. She picks up a maga-zine from the small table next to Suesetta's bed. "Your family gets *Ebony* magazine? Not fair!" Her eyes are full of wonder and envy. She holds the magazine with care. "You're so lucky, Suesetta. *Ebony* is so much better than *Negro Digest*."

"*Negro Digest* is smaller, but it has a lot of neat articles. I like it," Suesetta says.

"Yeah, but it's boring. This has lots more color and photos, fashion and cute boys."

We all start giggling.

I don't have much of an opinion because I've never read either. *Negro Digest* costs twenty-five cents, and Ollie Mae says there are twenty-five other things she could spend that money on, so we don't get any magazines.

꙳

We spend the next hour turning pages and pointing out who we think is cute, which outfits we are going to get, and which hairstyles we will wear. I stare at the spread that's right in the middle of the magazine. "Ooh, I'm going there," I tell them. "Rose-Meta House of Beauty in New York City! One day I'm going there to get my hair done," I say. "Can you imagine all of us getting our hair done in Harlem?"

We read the article out loud, taking turns. Phyllis goes first. She reads the headline. "Rose-Meta House of Beauty Biggest Negro Salon in the World."

Then me. "Rose-Meta opposes the idea that kinky hair is inferior. Her philosophy is that there is beauty in everyone," I read. There's a quote right next to a photo of a hairdresser pressing a woman's long, thick black hair— hair like mine. I read the rest of it. "No Negro hair is 'bad,' all Negro hair is attractive."

"Look at those curls!" Suesetta says. We look at the picture on the right side of the page. A woman has some pink rollers in her hair and a sea of curls hangs down to the sides of her face.

Suesetta reads the next part. "The luxurious Harlem beauty salon offers pink champagne and is so popular people come all the way from the South, Chicago, and Detroit—"

"See! I'm going one day," I tell them. "Told you."

They smile at me, but not like they believe this dream of mine will ever come true. They smile at me like I sometimes smile at Shirley and Jimmie when their jokes aren't funny but I have to be a good big sister and laugh anyway.

Suesetta jumps off the bed, says, "Want to bake some cookies?" She walks into the hallway, down the stairs, and to the kitchen. Phyllis and I follow her. Phyllis is still holding the magazine and plops down once we get to the kitchen table. She does a lot more reading while Suesetta and I do the mixing and the placing of cookie dough on the baking trays and into the oven.

We sit together at the table, waiting and waiting for the

cookies to bake. Suesetta and Phyllis start talking about a girl I don't know and I get lost following the gossip, so I pick up the magazine and turn the pages. I'm not really reading anything, just looking at the pictures. I stop at an ad that says, "Is Your Skin Dark, Dreadful, and Unattractive? So was mine." The woman in the magazine has tan skin, like the inside of an almond, like Suesetta and Phyllis's skin. She is holding a bottle with a label on it that reads, "Miss Emma's Bleaching Cream: For a Lovelier, Lighter Complexion." At the corner of the page there's a picture of the same woman before she used the cream. Her skin is brown, not tan.

I flip back to the spread about Miss Rose-Meta and her beauty salon in Harlem. I look at all the women sitting in the chair getting their hair straightened, curled, cut, and pinned up. All of them are tan.

I'm so distracted that I don't realize Phyllis is talking to me. "Betty, you hear me? Next Sunday we're going to style each other's hair, okay? We can each take turns being Miss Rose-Meta."

I close the magazine. "Okay."

The front door opens and Suesetta's family comes in, Uncle Clyde in the front with the rest of his family following behind him. Aunt Nina is holding baby Allen, who is a ball of sleep cuddled up against her chest.

Kay joins us in the kitchen and I'm not sure if she really wants to or not, but I guess being with us is better than playing with her little sister. She sits next to me at the kitchen table and picks up the magazine, flipping through it while we talk.

"Do you like living here?" I ask.

Kay pauses and takes a moment before answering. "Sure, I guess," Kay says. "Except for how cold it gets."

"Do you miss Alabama?" I ask. I'm wondering if maybe, like me, she left behind people and places that she holds on to in her dreams at night.

Kay says, "Of course. I miss my friends and my teachers. It's nice here, but in the South there's more country land than there are houses. Here, there are so many people and cars everywhere you turn. And the houses are so close to one another."

The timer dings, announcing that the cookies are ready.

Suesetta opens the oven. "They smell *sooo* good."

Kay pours milk and we eat our chocolate chip cookies without waiting for them to cool.

Our mouths are full and there's no more talking for a while. Everyone is enjoying the cookies. I don't bother to bring up the ad about a lighter, lovelier complexion. Don't ask Suesetta or Phyllis or Kay if they noticed that none of the girls in the magazine are brown. Like me.

Four

THE REST OF NOVEMBER GOES BY EXTRA SLOW
because I've been on punishment the entire month. On top
of getting a whipping, my consequence for leaving church
to get candy was that besides doing my own chores, I have
to do Shirley's and Jimmie's, too. The worst part of being on
punishment isn't the cleaning up and washing dishes and
raking leaves, it's not being able to go over to Suesetta's
house after church. I see Suesetta and Phyllis at school,
though, so I guess it could be a whole lot worse.

Today, my home economics teacher is teaching us how
to sew aprons. So far in Mrs. Collins's class, we've learned
about the different components that make a sewing machine

work and how to use it. "For the next few weeks," she says, "you'll learn stitching techniques. How to hem, how to sew a band, and how to make pockets," she tells us.

Phyllis raises her hand. "Why do we have to learn how to sew?"

Mrs. Collins smiles and picks up a thin piece of fabric from her desk and holds it up. "Why? To be able to design something with your mind and your hands is a powerful skill to have. It's your own creation. Who wouldn't want to know how to do that?"

Phyllis sits back in her seat, looking perplexed by Mrs. Collins. But I lean forward.

❧

After school, I go home and do my homework right away. Mrs. Malloy is coming to pick me up for choir rehearsal. It's the only non-school activity I've been able to do all month, and only because it's church-related. When Mrs. Malloy comes for me, she sends Suesetta to the door. Ollie Mae tells me, "Your punishment ends tomorrow and not a moment sooner. I want you to come straight home after rehearsal, Betty Dean."

"Yes, ma'am," I promise.

She closes the door.

When rehearsal is over, I go straight downstairs to find Mrs. Malloy. She is in the church office with Mrs. Peck. "We're ready," I tell her.

"Okay, sweetheart. We're finishing up these packets. Just give me a few more minutes," she says. "In fact, if you and Suesetta help us we can finish sooner." She picks up a stack of flyers with one hand and registration forms with the other. "Here, staple a registration form to each flyer," she tells me. She calls up to Suesetta and gives her a different stack of papers and a handful of envelopes. "These are letters to send to our other chapters," Mrs. Malloy says. "You can stuff the envelopes."

"Other cities have a Housewives' League, too?" Suesetta asks.

Mrs. Peck tells us, "Yes, we're all over the nation and still growing strong, ladies."

Mrs. Malloy looks at me and says, "You know, there are junior members all over the nation, too."

"Yes, Suesetta told me," I tell her.

Mrs. Peck and Mrs. Malloy have looks on their faces like they expect me to say more. I look at Suesetta, who won't look up no matter how hard I stare at her. I'm not joining if she's not joining, and since she isn't saying anything, I just keep quiet.

Mrs. Peck smiles at Mrs. Malloy and it feels like they just passed a secret to each other. "Let us know if you have any questions about joining, Betty," Mrs. Malloy says.

"Yes, ma'am. I will."

Then Mrs. Malloy checks her watch and says, "My, it's later than I thought. I better get you girls home. You have school tomorrow."

❧

The whole way home, Suesetta and I talk about what we want for Christmas and what we're going to buy as gifts for our family and friends. Suesetta has a long list—something for her parents, for Aunt Nina and Uncle Clyde, for baby Allen, Bernice, and Kay.

I ask her, "Where are you going to get enough money to buy all those gifts?"

"I get an allowance for doing chores," Suesetta says.

"You get paid to do housework?"

"Yes. Don't you?"

"No. Ollie Mae would never pay us for cleaning up," I tell her. "Never."

"Well, how are you going to have money to buy gifts?"

"We usually pull names and Arthur gives each of us enough to get one person in the family something special. That way everybody has a gift under the tree."

We stop at a red light. I don't know what time it is and am starting to fear that Ollie Mae will be upset that I am getting home later than usual. I think about Suesetta's family and how she'll have enough money to buy something for everyone and how she had enough money to get candy without having to use her offering. And I wonder what I can do to have my own money so I don't always have to ask Ollie Mae for it.

The light changes and we drive two more blocks, passing Mr. Malloy's shoe repair store. There's a sign in the window that says HELP WANTED. I doubt Mr. Malloy would hire a sixth grader, but it won't hurt to ask. Not that I know anything about fixing shoes, but the sign says HELP, so maybe I wouldn't have to know that much. I lean forward to make sure Mrs. Malloy can hear me and ask, "What kind of help does Mr. Malloy need at his store?"

"Oh, just someone to log inventory and keep the store-room and display shelves clean and organized."

I could do that. I don't say more because there's no point in asking before I get permission from Ollie Mae, but I sure hope he doesn't find someone else before I get the chance.

Mrs. Malloy pulls up to my house and parks. But she leaves the car running. "I'll be right back," she tells Sue-setta. "Betty, I'd like to apologize to your mom for bringing you home after curfew and let her know you were helping me at the church."

I say goodbye to Suesetta, and when Mrs. Malloy and I get to my door, Ollie Mae opens it before I even knock. "You're late," she says.

Mrs. Malloy apologizes before Ollie Mae can say

anything else. In just a few sentences she's erased the frown on Ollie Mae's face and the two of them stand in the doorway talking about coupons and sales and Christmas shopping. Mrs. Malloy gives me a hug and a kiss on my forehead and leaves. I think maybe Mrs. Malloy has some kind of miracle-working power, because she just put out the fire that was in Ollie Mae's eyes.

Ollie Mae closes the door and says, "We already ate supper. I put a plate aside for you."

I go into the kitchen. The house is quiet, which means everyone else is already in bed.

I hadn't realized how hungry I am until I smell the fried chicken, string beans, macaroni and cheese, and homemade dinner rolls. Ollie Mae makes the best dinner rolls from scratch—sweet and buttery.

I sit at the small kitchen table. Ollie Mae stands at the sink, washing dishes.

Here we are, not talking. Just the sound of fork clanking against plate, water splashing against pot.

"Mr. Malloy needs help at his shoe repair store," I say.

Ollie Mae doesn't say anything. She just washes dishes,

her back to me, the running water filling the silence. She rinses dishes, puts them in the rack to dry.

"Just simple things like keeping track of inventory and making the shelves neat," I explain.

"Uh-huh."

"I was thinking, with Christmas coming, maybe I could work there and earn money," I tell her. "I wouldn't spend it all on gifts, though. I would save some, too."

"I'll think about it," Ollie Mae says.

Mrs. Malloy is definitely a miracle worker.

"I was also thinking about joining the junior Housewives' League. Well, if Suesetta joins. I don't want to do it by myself," I tell her.

She doesn't say anything.

"I think it would be fun to get all dressed up and go to the fancy fund-raising banquets. Sometimes really important people are at those events. I think it would be fun to—"

"How do you think you'll keep up with your schoolwork and chores if you're at choir practice, the shoe store, and the Housewives' League?" Ollie Mae asks.

"I'll manage. I won't let it get in the way of my studies."

"Hmm," Ollie Mae says. She rinses more dishes. "You sure are spending a lot of time with Mrs. Malloy. You really like her, huh?"

"Yes, ma'am, I do."

"What do you like about her?" Ollie Mae asks.

I swallow my last bite of macaroni and cheese. I could go on and on about all the things I like about Mrs. Malloy. I like that when I'm talking to her, she looks me in the eyes and really listens. That she'd stop washing dishes, just for one moment, and ask me how my day was. I like that she's doing something for our community and standing up for what's right.

But instead of listing the reasons, I just say, "Everything, I guess."

"Everything, huh?" Ollie Mae shuts the water off, turns, and faces me. She wipes her wet hands on her apron, looking at me long and hard with those apologizing eyes. The two of us sit in silence, both of us knowing I may never say that about her.

Five

CHRISTMAS IS NEXT WEEK.

I am at Suesetta's house, sitting on her bed, waiting for Kay to get ready so we can all go shopping at J.L.'s. Kay is in front of the mirror, doing her hair and painting her face like we are going someplace other than a department store. "I hope I can find a cute pair of shoes today," Kay says, even though there's a row of shoes lined up against the wall, stretching from one end to the next, that all belong to her.

Suesetta and I need to finish getting our Christmas gifts. I have something for everyone on my list except Shirley. We don't normally shop at J.L.'s, but Kay saw an advertisement about a holiday sale at Toytown, so we are going to shop for Shirley and Bernice.

Ollie Mae actually said yes to me working for Mr. Malloy, but only twice a week and only if I keep my grades up. She said no to me joining the Housewives' League, but I'm not too upset about that. I haven't even convinced Suesetta to join yet, and the more I think about it, going door-to-door in the cold isn't the best way to spend a Saturday.

Finally, after fifteen more minutes of waiting, Kay says, "Okay, I'm ready."

We head outside and walk down the block to the trolley. We get on the line headed in the direction of J.L.'s and go straight to the back of the car. The closer we get to J.L.'s, the more white folk get on. Once we arrive, there are hardly any Negroes in sight. The people shopping, the people working behind the counter, the models in the advertisements—all white.

The only people who aren't white are the ones operating the elevators. Kay says, "You two stay close to me, okay?"

Walking through J.L.'s, I notice all the white people

looking at us. But they quickly look away to avoid meeting our eyes, except for the little girl who is staring at me right now. She is holding on to her mother's hand, eyes big and looking right at me. I wave. She looks away, too, like she didn't even see me saying hello.

When we get to Toytown, we stare inside the display windows. There's a whole Christmas scene with a train riding around a snowy track. I see all the miniature townsmen and townswomen stationed throughout this imaginary village. All of the figurines are white. Not one Negro.

We walk into the store. I try not to notice if anyone is looking at us. I just keep my eyes focused on the toys, trying to find the aisle where I can get a play tea set for Shirley. "There they are!" Suesetta shouts. She is pointing to a long shelf ahead of us. There are all kinds of tea sets displayed. I choose the set that has enough dishes for me, Shirley, Jimmie, Juanita, and even Juanita's imaginary friend to each have our tea. Kay helps me get the box down and Suesetta grabs one, too, for Bernice.

As we wait our turn at the register, a white woman steps in front of us. At first I think maybe she is passing through to get to the other side of this crowded store, but she sets her items down on the cash register counter. I look up at Kay, who is looking furious but not saying anything.

I want her to say something. *I* want to say something. I want to say, *Excuse me, ma'am, but we're standing here. Don't you see us?*

The woman pays for her things, collects her shopping bags from the clerk, and walks out of the store, not looking back, not even thanking us for letting her cut in front of us.

The man at the counter doesn't speak or look us in the eye. He doesn't make small talk with us about the weather, like he did with the woman. When I pay him, he takes my money and that's it. No *Thank you*. No *Merry Christmas*. Nothing. I take my bag without saying thank you and Kay nudges me. "Mind your manners," she whispers.

"Thank you, sir," I mumble.

He just looks at me.

We walk away.

"They were rude," I say. "That woman just stood in front of us like we were invisible—and that man didn't even say thank you."

Kay and Suesetta don't say anything.

"Don't you think they were rude?"

"Yes," Kay says. "But that's just the way they are. You know that."

"Yeah, Betty, what did you expect?" Suesetta asks.

I don't know what I expected. I just know that I want to leave this place right now. I think maybe coming to J.L.'s was the worst idea ever. I think about Mrs. Peck and Mrs. Malloy and the Housewives' League. They are right. We wouldn't be treated like this in the Negro community.

Kay says, "Just one more stop and then we can go." She points to a shoe store.

"Do we have to?" I ask. It's not like she really *needs* another pair of shoes.

"I'll be quick," Kay says. "I just want to look."

We walk over to the area where people are trying on shoes and Kay stops in the middle of the aisle. "These are so pretty," she says.

Kay reaches for a pair of strappy black suede heels and before her hand touches them, a white clerk grabs the shoes. "Interested in trying these on?" she asks.

"Yes, ma'am," Kay says.

So much for just looking.

She sits down on the chair next to a white woman who is also trying on shoes.

"Do you have your shoe insert?" the store clerk asks.

"My shoe insert?"

The woman gives us a look like we should know what she's talking about. I look around and notice a Negro woman who has a small child with her. The little boy has his shoe off and his mother is putting cardboard cutouts of his feet into the shoes he wants to try on. The store clerk points. "You can't try on shoes unless you use shoe inserts," she tells us.

I can see that this rule doesn't apply to everyone because the white woman next to us is trying on a pair of high heels in her bare feet.

"Do you have shoe inserts?" the store clerk asks again.

Kay looks down at the floor and her voice dissolves into a soft vapor. "No, ma'am. No, I don't."

"Well, I can't let you try on shoes," the woman says.

Kay stands, looks at me and Suesetta, and says, "Come on. Let's go."

I don't move. "But this isn't fair—"

"Betty, let's go," Kay says.

"But—"

"Betty."

We walk out of the shoe store, none of us saying a word. Kay walks with her head down. Suesetta, too. We go outside, wait for the trolley, hop on board, pay our money, take our seats. It isn't until we are walking to Suesetta's that I break the silence and say, "We have nothing to feel bad about. That wasn't fair, and they don't deserve our money anyway if we can't even try on their shoes."

My heart is throbbing. I can't stop thinking about all those people who were looking at us, like our feelings didn't matter. The store clerk who wouldn't let Kay try on shoes because she didn't have a silly piece of cardboard. The woman who stepped in front of us, walking through us like we were wafts of smoke. The way the man took my money and didn't even wish me a nice day.

I think about the Housewives' League and how what they are doing isn't just about coupons or extravagant banquets, but about not wanting any of us to ever walk into a store and not be greeted in a courteous manner or treated with dignity, like human beings.

I turn to Suesetta and before I can even say anything, she says, "I'll join with you."

Now all I have to do is convince Ollie Mae.

Six

I CAN'T SLEEP. JUANITA AND I HAVE BEEN BACK
in bed for a while now. She is snoring, and for once, Shirley is
on her side of the bed. I close my eyes, try to stop my mind
from wandering, but it is skipping from memory to memory.

Summer days with my Aunt Fannie Mae.

Country rain showers and magnolia flowers.

My Grandma Matilda and her pecan trees.

Lynched bodies dangling in the country breeze.

Detroit.

Ollie Mae.

Mrs. Malloy.

Bethel AME Church.

Pastor Peck.

Pastor Dames.

Suesetta and Phyllis.

Toytown.

Shoe inserts.

The Housewives' League.

Ebony magazine.

Billy Eckstine.

Straight hair.

Brown skin.

I roll over, try to find a more comfortable position so I can sleep. But instead, more thoughts, more questions, more memories.

I think back to two years ago, 1943.

Detroit was having some kind of war. But Ollie Mae and Arthur wouldn't talk to us about it.

At church one week, the deacons were praying to the Lord for peace, and Mrs. Duncan and a few other ladies cried through the entire service. Every prayer prayed that Sunday was asking the Lord to end the world's war overseas and to stop the race riot against Negroes right here in America, and to bring innocent family members back home from jail alive.

I remember that at the end of service, the congregation took up a collection for Mrs. Duncan. Her son, Roger, had been killed during the riots, and she needed help paying for his funeral. I didn't go to the funeral, but I know that Mrs. Duncan hasn't looked the same since she buried her son. She smiles sometimes, but not like she used to. She still shouts out "Thank you, Jesus" every now and then, but it doesn't sound the same. Sounds like a person who is saying thank you to be polite, not because they are really grateful.

Not long after that, I found Arthur's newspaper on the table in the kitchen. It was full of pictures showing Detroit on fire, Detroit in a rage. A car was turned on its side, flames rising to the sky like the burning bush we learned about in Sunday school.

There was a photograph of a colored man being attacked by a white mob in the middle of the street. There were so many of them, but the colored man was all by himself, had no one to protect him. Looked like two police officers were escorting him to get through the mob. But it was hard to tell who the policemen were actually helping.

Other pages of the newspaper had photographs of burning buildings, boarded-up stores, and desolate streets.

At the top of the page, the headline was printed in real big letters. I read it slow. Sounded out each word. "Race Riots Kill More than 20, Injure 700."

"Why are all the grownups fighting?" I asked. I didn't even mean to say it out loud.

Ollie Mae must have heard me, because she appeared out of nowhere and snatched the newspaper right out of my hands. "You have enough years ahead of you to know pain, Betty Dean." She tore the newspaper into pieces, threw it away. It was the first time I ever saw tears in Ollie Mae's eyes. She didn't let any of them fall, but I saw them gathering. I heard the way she took a deep breath, then released it, then took one more. I saw her keep her back to me, wipe her face, then turn around and keep on going like nothing was bothering her at all. And all I could think about for days after was, *Where do uncried tears go?*

I remember wanting to take the torn pieces of newspaper out of the garbage, put all of the letters back together to make words again. People died. Didn't seem right to bury their stories in the trash.

Ollie Mae couldn't really keep me from knowing what

was going on, not with Arthur listening to the radio every morning before he left for work. He'd sit right in front of it with his coffee and listen to the news. The radio was made of dark-brown wood, square with three knobs at the bottom. One knob to change the station, one to adjust the sound, and the other to turn it on or off.

I lie in bed thinking about those days when the streets smelled like smoke and ash, when the stores where we'd just bought candy were closed and all boarded up. Ollie Mae just kept living like people weren't dying outside our door.

I remember one Sunday, Mrs. Malloy stood at the podium at the end of service. She led the congregation in prayer, asking the Lord to comfort all the families who had lost loved ones in the protests and riots. She pleaded with everyone to come together and to volunteer to clean up the neighborhoods and help restore the Negro businesses that had been destroyed. She said we must not allow fear to keep us at home. She said we need the support of one another. The ushers began passing out volunteer sheets. Ollie Mae and Arthur didn't sign up. So that meant I couldn't either, but I wanted to. I really wanted to.

Seven

CHRISTMAS IS HERE AND INSTEAD OF A snow-covered ground, the streets are one big ice-skating rink. Freezing rain fell all last night, so now icicles are hanging off of tree branches like crystals and all the houses on the block look like they are made of glass.

The best part of today is watching Shirley, Jimmie, and Juanita play with the tea set. They are taking turns pouring pretend tea into the tiny plastic cups. Shirley is fussing at Jimmie and Juanita for drinking too fast. "It's hot, you have to sip it," she says.

Ollie Mae got me a Singer sewing machine. It is just what I wanted. This way, I can practice sewing at home and not just at school. Mrs. Collins says I am a fast learner, that she wants me to help some of the other girls in class. I've been sewing all afternoon, practicing making pockets and handkerchiefs so I can work on getting the stitching perfectly straight. I can't wait to tell Mrs. Collins that now, I'll be even better at helping others in class.

Ollie Mae comes into the living room and starts cleaning up all of the crumpled Christmas wrapping paper and empty boxes that were left behind from this morning's gift opening. She looks over my shoulder, watches me sew for a bit. "My, you *are* good," she says. "I couldn't sew that well when I was your age."

"Really? How did you get so good at it, then?" I ask. Ollie Mae is the best at making quilts. Whenever a woman at the church has a baby, she makes a quilt for them. Sometimes people pay her to do it.

"Practice," Ollie Mae says. "The more you work at it, the better you get."

"Mrs. Collins says sewing is masterful because it means you can make something out of nothing."

"Hmm. I never thought of it like that. Just something

I had to learn how to do," Ollie Mae tells me. "Growing up, everyone did it. Sewing was a way to save money. We were self-sufficient."

"Did people sew their own clothes so they wouldn't have to buy from white folk?"

"Betty Dean, now you hush up all that talk. I told you that you are not joining that Housewives' League. You are already too busy and—"

"I wasn't asking to join. I was just asking—"

"Are you sassing me, child?"

"No, ma'am. I'm just explaining that—"

"Sure sounds like you're talking back," Ollie Mae says.

I don't understand what I did wrong, what I said to get Ollie Mae so upset. I just keep sewing, stop trying to explain myself, stop talking. The needle stomps along the fabric, its steady *thump thump thump* the only sound in the room.

Then Ollie Mae says, "I get you a sewing machine and all you want to do is talk about Mrs. Collins this and Mrs. Peck that, and Mrs. Malloy said this and that. Here I am cleaning up and you haven't even offered to help, like

I haven't taught you good manners. Don't you see all this paper on the floor, Betty Dean?"

"But I didn't make that mess. I already threw away my—"

"Stop talking back. You hear?"

Sometimes I forget that Ollie Mae's questions aren't meant to be answered.

Arthur calls out from the kitchen, "You two stop all that fussing. It's Christmas. Can we have some peace in this house?"

I keep sewing, keep listening to the needle run and run. I think of running away, running away from Ollie Mae.

I keep on sewing, keep on being masterful.

I am almost finished with the handkerchief. I will get up and help Ollie Mae as soon as I'm done, even though the mess was made by Sonny, Henry, Shirley, and Jimmie. I don't understand why she's not fussing at any of them for not helping her clean. Why is she always picking on me?

Ollie Mae comes over and orders me to stop sewing. "Get up and help me now, Betty Dean," she says.

I don't tell her that I was about to get up, that I really want to help her. That I want to do whatever it takes so she is not mad at me. That I will do anything to make her like me the way she likes my sisters.

As I help her clean up the living room, Ollie Mae tells me how ungrateful I am. That I am an ornery little girl. That I am like my daddy, bad to the core. I don't say anything. And even though there is no more sound from the running needle, I still hear it in my heart and it hurts. I see myself running. Running so fast. Running away from her.

Eight

TONIGHT, I AM NOT ASKING GOD ANYTHING.

Tonight, I am listening to the rain fall, listening to the wind whistle, to Shirley's breaths and Jimmie's snores, to Juanita's tossing and turning, and to the *tick tick tick* of the clock.

I am listening for Aunt Fannie Mae's laugh and Grandma Matilda's singing and the creak of the swing in the backyard that swayed under my favorite tree.

I am listening. No questions tonight.

Just listening and waiting and hoping that if I keep quiet for once, maybe God will speak to me.

Nine

THE ICE HAS MELTED, AND STILL NO SNOW. Arthur can't stop complaining because every winter he takes Sonny and Henry outside to sled down the driveway. There hasn't been enough snow for them to sled even once.

It's the last Saturday of 1945. In three days, it will be a new year and Ollie Mae will take the Christmas tree down and we'll all share our New Year's resolutions and Arthur will lead us in prayer, like he does every year. Shirley, Jimmie, and I are in the living room talking about what our resolutions are going to be. Shirley and Jimmie are spread across the rug on the living room floor, lying on their bellies, coloring, their crayons scattered around them. I am sitting at my sewing table.

Shirley says, "Maybe this year I will learn one hundred scriptures by heart."

"That's impossible," Jimmie says.

"Is not," Shirley yells. She looks at me, asking me to take her side.

"It's not impossible, Jimmie. Just challenging."

"See," Shirley says.

The phone rings and Arthur answers it. As soon as I hear him say, "Well, hello, Suesetta," I get up and go into the kitchen. "It's for you," he tells me.

Suesetta is calling to ask if I can come over. When I ask Ollie Mae, she says, "I don't mind, but these dishes need to be washed first."

I tell Suesetta I'll be over soon.

When I hang up the phone, Ollie Mae says, "I'm going to the market."

"Okay," I say. I stand in front of the sink and look at all of the dishes that I have to wash. With all of us here for lunch today, it looks like every dish in our house is in the sink—pots and pans, plates, bowls, glasses, silverware.

I know that Suesetta is waiting for me and there's no telling how long it will take for all of these dishes to get washed, dried, and put away. I go back into the living room to find Shirley. I am very careful about how I word my question. "Shirley, the dishes need to be washed. Can you do them?"

Shirley puts her orange crayon down. "Now?" she asks.

"They need to be done before Ollie Mae gets back."

"Okay," she says. And just like that I've found a way to get what I want *and* make Ollie Mae happy. She didn't say *I* have to wash the dishes myself. She just said they need to get washed.

"I'm going to Suesetta's," I tell Shirley. "I'm going to stop by the candy store on my way back. I'll bring you back some Sugar Daddies, okay?"

Shirley smiles real big when I say this, and I think I could probably get her to do anything now.

❦

I stay at Suesetta's for a few hours. We do homework, listen to records, experiment with Kay's makeup, and then go to the candy store so I can get Shirley her Sugar Daddies like I promised. When I get home it only takes one minute for me to know something is wrong. Shirley is sitting on the sofa with red eyes. When I look at her and ask, "What happened?" she shifts her eyes to the kitchen, where Ollie Mae is cooking. Arthur is still sitting at the radio listening to *Amos 'n' Andy*, not even paying attention to Sonny and Henry, who are tearing apart Jimmie's dolly.

I snatch it from them on my way to the kitchen, tell them to go play in their room. I step into the kitchen. "I'm home," I announce.

Ollie Mae is at the stove stirring a pot. She turns around, says, "Where'd you learn to be so dishonest?"

She wipes her hands on her apron and walks toward me.

"What did I do?"

"Didn't I ask you to wash the dishes?"

"No," I tell Ollie Mae. "You said the dishes needed to get washed, so I asked Shirley to do them."

"Don't sass me, child. You think you're smarter than me? You know I intended for you to wash those dishes. And you made your sister do your work." Ollie Mae is yelling now. "You think you don't have to listen to my rules in my house?"

"No, ma'am, I—"

"Don't you talk back to me, child." She grabs the switch she had waiting and starts whipping me with it. I lean back against the wall. I hold my arms up to protect myself.

Now, my sisters and even Arthur are in the kitchen. Arthur says, "Ollie Mae, that's enough. Leave that child alone."

Ollie Mae seems to come out of a trance when she hears Arthur's voice. She turns and walks away.

I slide down the wall, sit on the floor taking in deep breaths. My sisters and my brothers gather around me, telling me not to cry and that I'll be okay. Ollie Mae orders them to the table. And I think I know who left that bruise on me when I was just a baby learning how to say *Momma*.

I go to my room, stay in there while everyone else eats dinner. Ollie Mae probably thinks I'm in here crying, that I am feeling bad for talking back to her.

But she's wrong. I am not letting any tears fall. I am not feeling bad at all.

I am packing.

I pack enough clothes to last for two days and leave for Suesetta's house. Arthur tries to stop me but Ollie Mae says, "Let her go."

I hug Shirley, Jimmie, and Juanita and when they squeeze me, I realize how sore I am. I push out a smile, say bye to Sonny and Henry, and I leave.

I've walked this route to Suesetta's so many times, but this evening it feels longer. It's colder now that night is coming. Once I get to Suesetta's doorstep, I drop the bag at my feet and let my arm rest. I knock. Twice. No one answers. I look next door at the Malloys' house, but the lights are all off and their car is not in the driveway. I sit on Suesetta's porch and wait.

The moon hovers over me, keeping me company. I see headlights down the block and then, out of the night fog, I see the Malloys driving onto the street. Their headlights wash over me as Mr. Malloy parks in front of his house. He doesn't even have the car turned off before Mrs. Malloy is out of the car and running over. She doesn't ask me any questions, she just picks up my bag, says, "Come on, baby." As we walk over to her house, all the tears I've been holding in fall. Mrs. Malloy takes my hand. Holds it tight like my Aunt Fannie Mae did, like she's never going to let me go.

Right after I step inside Mrs. Malloy's house, she takes off my coat and we sit on the sofa in her living room. She looks at the welts on my arms and the first thing she says to me is, "Now, let's see what we can do about these tears." She pulls a tissue from a fancy tissue box and dabs my eyes, but the more she wipes, the more tears flow. And I feel like some kind of fool crying and not being able to say anything. I think, *She'll never have me back in her home.* But not even that thought can keep me from becoming a puddle in Mrs. Malloy's arms. She rocks me from side to side, holding me tight. I couldn't get out of her embrace even if I wanted to. "It's okay, baby. Go ahead and let it all out. Let it all out," she says. And when she says *all*, I realize I am not crying just about what happened tonight, but about everything that's ever happened in my whole entire life.

At first the tears come out heavy like a blizzard. But the more she holds and rocks me, my chest stops heaving up and down and I settle into her arms. Then the tears fall gentle like tiny snowflakes. The kind that don't stick to the ground.

Mrs. Malloy tips my chin up and looks me in my eyes. "You're a strong girl, Betty. You know that?"

I nod, even though I have never thought of myself as strong. Most times I only hear the word *strong* when Arthur is talking to Sonny or Henry about the heavyweight champion of the world, Joe Louis, or some other boxer he loves. He boxes with them in the living room, and every single time he lets them win. And when they are done, he holds up their arms, one by one, and feels for their muscles. "I've got some strong sons," he always says. And they flex their pint-size muscles around the house for the rest of the afternoon.

And then there are the times when one of the deacons makes an announcement at the end of service: "We need a few strong men to help carry the chairs."

But never, ever have I heard the word *strong* applied to me.

Mrs. Malloy shows me around the house, to a room that has a bed covered with the most beautiful quilt I've ever seen. Every square has its own unique design. The outer border is purple, and there are lavender pillows propped up against the headboard. Mr. Malloy has already brought my bag in. "This is your room," she tells me, and she says it like what she means is this is my room forever. "Make yourself at home."

"Have you eaten yet?" Mrs. Malloy asks me a moment later. "Let's get you some supper."

"I'm not hungry, ma'am." I think of the feast in the oven that Ollie Mae was baking. The pot roast, collard greens, sweet potatoes, and baked apple pie. Think of Shirley, Jimmie, and Juanita all sitting at the table eating and talking and making faces at Henry and Sonny when Ollie Mae isn't looking. I wonder if they've asked where I am.

Mrs. Malloy goes into the kitchen, motioning for me to follow her. "You can't go to bed on an empty stomach," she says. She opens a cupboard and takes out Velvet Peanut Butter and spreads it on a slice of bread. Mr. Malloy warms a small pot of milk and honey, then pours it into a glass for me. I eat just half of the sandwich and sip the entire glass of sweet milk.

When I am finished, we pray together. Mr. Malloy prays for Ollie Mae. Asks God to touch her heart. I open my eyes. Look at him and Mrs. Malloy and wonder if their prayer will help Ollie Mae want me as much as I want her.

Then Mr. Malloy prays, "And heal her, Lord, from whatever is hurting her." And I wonder what Ollie Mae could be hurting from.

After prayer, we say good night to each other and go to our rooms. At first when I get in the bed, I stay to the right side, bundling and tucking my aching arms and legs in a cocoon like I always do to make room for Shirley. But then I remember that it's just me sleeping in this bed, and so I stretch my whole body out, make an X with my aching limbs open wide and centered in the middle of the mattress like a snow angel all alone.

It doesn't take me long to fall asleep, but then I wake up in the middle of the night. I sit straight up, my heart thumping and thumping. *Who's going to take Juanita to the bathroom when she wakes up?*

I don't sleep for the rest of the night.

Detroit, Michigan
1946

When I sing, trouble can sit right on my
shoulder and I don't even notice.
—Sarah Vaughan

Ten

I'VE BEEN STAYING WITH MRS. MALLOY FOR almost a month now. One night turned into another night, and then a week went by, and another, and another. Mrs. Malloy went over to Ollie Mae's to pick up more clothes for me. She even brought back a few things from my bedroom to help make the guest room feel more familiar.

I am not used to having this much space in a bed. Having my own room means I get to spread out and the cover is all mine. I get to decorate and put things where I like them. I have privacy to try on a new dress and twirl in the mirror to see if I like it. I can even do my homework without distractions, play records, dance, and sing along to my favorite songs.

But it also means that I don't have my sisters with me at night to talk to and laugh with. They are not there when a noise frightens me. I don't have someone's hand to hold as I tiptoe to the window, only to realize the scary noise is just a branch scraping the glass, just the wind.

It is Saturday morning and I wake to the sound of Ollie Mae's voice. For a moment, I am confused about where I am. I have not heard her voice in the morning for twenty-six days. We see each other at church, but all she does is look at me with those eyes that tell me she doesn't love me like I want her to.

I wonder why she is here. Maybe she misses me after all. Maybe she is sorry and wants me to come back home.

I sit up in my bed when I hear Mrs. Malloy saying, "Let me take her off your hands, Ollie Mae. I don't mind at all. She can live here with us."

I tiptoe to the door, don't open it. Just press my ear against the frame.

Ollie Mae asks, "And what are you going to do when you get tired of her?"

"I won't get tired of her, dear."

"Are you sure? If she doesn't come home with me now, she never will."

"Yes," Mrs. Malloy says. "I *want* her."

Ollie Mae's voice has no emotion. "Well, you can have her. She's yours."

Just like that.

"I'll have the rest of her belongings packed by noon," Ollie Mae says.

"I'll have my husband pick them up," Mrs. Malloy says.

The front door creaks open and then closes.

I step out of the bedroom and join Mrs. Malloy, who is in the kitchen filling a teakettle with water.

I don't know what to say. I want to cry, I want to say thank you. I want to run out the door, yell at Ollie Mae, ask her, *What have I done for you to just give me away—twice? Why don't you love me?* But instead, I sit at the kitchen table and breathe. I control every breath of air I take. In and out, in and out.

As I exhale, Mrs. Malloy sets the kettle on the stove. She takes two teacups from the cabinet and puts one cube of sugar in each.

"I wish I could hate her," I whisper. If I hated Ollie Mae, maybe I wouldn't care so much that she can't love me like I want her to. Maybe I should be happy that someone else can, but instead I am sitting here feeling like my heart has a million welts on it, stinging and burning.

The kettle whistles and Mrs. Malloy pours our tea.

"I really wish I could hate her," I say again.

Mrs. Malloy sits across from me, says, "Betty, there are a lot of reasons for you to be upset and confused. But, sweetheart, the easy thing to do is to hold on to disappointment and pain. The hard thing to do is to let it go and forgive. The Lord has a plan for you that's bigger than you can ever imagine. Right now you just have to have faith in the Lord and find the good and praise it. Count your blessings, young lady. Name them one by one—even the small things. Doing that will comfort your heart, it will comfort your soul."

I listen to Mrs. Malloy's words as I breathe in and out,

in and out. I nod to let her know I understand what she is saying. I know I have a lot to be grateful for, I do. But right now I can't think about anything except my mother, who left me. She didn't even ask to see me.

I bite the inside of my lip, try to keep these tears from falling because I don't like to cry in front of people. I don't want Mrs. Malloy to think I don't appreciate all she is doing for me. I don't want her to give me away, too. I can't sit here and count blessings, can't stop the sadness from rising in my chest.

Mrs. Malloy drinks more of her tea, but my cup is still full. I clear my throat, say, "Can the counting of my blessings start tomorrow?"

"Yes, Betty. It can." She reaches across the table and takes my hand.

Eleven

BY THE END OF THE DAY, ALL OF MY CLOTHES, my books, and my sewing machine are here at the Malloys'. I also have two framed photographs. One of me with Shirley, Jimmie, and Juanita, and the other with the entire family. Mr. Malloy got me a record player, so now Suesetta and Phyllis can come over and listen to music at my house.

This room is mine now, all mine.

Mrs. Malloy was right. Focusing on the good makes my heart hurt less. Tonight I am lying in my bed counting blessings, finding the good, and praising it.

A roof over my head.

Plenty of food to eat.

Pretty dresses, a warm coat.

And new shoes on my feet.

Books and magazines.

All the records of Billy Eckstine.

Shirley's kindness.

Jimmie's laugh.

Juanita's little hugs.

Suesetta and Phyllis and all the fun we have together.

Mrs. and Mr. Malloy's promise to keep me forever.

God, for always bringing someone into my life to love me when Ollie Mae's love isn't enough.

Twelve

THE NEXT DAY WE GO TO CHURCH, AND afterwards I spend time at Suesetta's. I've been here for an hour, and her baby cousin has been crying the whole time. Bernice and Kay are with me and Suesetta in her room. Kay is braiding Bernice's hair, and Bernice is flinching, saying "ouch" every five seconds.

When I tell Suesetta that I am living with Mrs. Malloy permanently, she is so excited about being neighbors that I don't think she even realizes that what I am saying is that my mother doesn't want me. "You mean, forever?" she asks.

"Yes. I live with them now."

"So we can keep walking home together after school?"

Suesetta asks without stopping for an answer. "And once we're in high school, we can take the trolley by ourselves and meet Phyllis on the way. And then we can go to college together, the three of us."

We have a whole nother year until high school, but Suesetta is always thinking about the next thing. Her mind is always peeking into the future.

Kay takes the comb and parts Bernice's hair so she can make a new ponytail. "Hold still, now," Kay says.

I flip through the latest issue of *Ebony* magazine, looking for a hairstyle. It takes me a while to find something that I think will look good on me. I bend the magazine back and show Suesetta a picture. "You think you can fix my bangs like this?" I ask.

"Yeah, that's pretty." She studies the picture, then touches my hair, squeezing it as if she's testing out the softness of a pillow. "I think so," she says.

Kay sticks the comb in Bernice's hair. She reaches for the magazine. "Let me see." She looks at the picture, then at my hair, then back at the picture, then back at my hair. "Yeah, your hair can do this. That will look good on you because you have high cheekbones. All we have to do is roll your hair real tight." She looks back at the magazine. "But to be sure, I think we should cut your hair in the front."

"Cut my hair?"

"Just the front. Your bangs are too long. That's why they won't stay curled."

"Ollie Mae doesn't want me cutting my hair," I tell Kay.

Kay says, "You don't live with her anymore, right?"

When she says this, I don't feel tears swelling or sadness in my heart. "Right," I say. "Go ahead."

Kay gets up from doing Bernice's hair, grabs scissors out of Suesetta's desk drawer, and stands in front of me, scissors in hand. She cups the front of my hair in her left hand. She puts the scissors down and picks up a comb to run through my hair.

"Are you sure you know what you're doing?" I ask.

She doesn't answer. Just picks the scissors back up, holds a section of my hair between two of her fingers and starts cutting. I close my eyes, hearing the *snip snip snip* of the scissors and feeling the thick clumps of long hair hit my nose, tickling me and making me sneeze.

"Be still!" Kay shouts.

"Can't help it."

Kay finishes cutting and she won't even let me look in the mirror. "It's not going to look good until I roll it," she says. She takes her small canister of Royal Crown Hair Dressing, dips her fingers into the pomade, and dabs it on my hair. Then she takes a thick pink sponge roller and twirls my hair onto the roller real slow, real tight, until it's rolled to my scalp. "There," she says. "Leave the roller in till tomorrow and it'll be curled tight." Kay places my cut hairs in the trash can. Then she goes back to braiding Bernice's hair.

I look in the mirror. I can't wait to take the roller out in the morning and see what having bangs will look like. Then I have another thought—that getting bangs is not the only new thing I'm going to do today.

I turn around to Suesetta and ask, "Are you ready to join the Housewives' League?"

Thirteen

SUESETTA AND I HAVE BEEN MEMBERS OF THE junior Housewives' League for a month now. So far, we've mostly helped with organizing packets that Mrs. Malloy mailed out, and we've started our young scholars class. Today is Saturday and the Housewives' League is passing out coupons and canvassing to sign up new members in Paradise Valley and Black Bottom. February's sky is gray and cloudy, but at least there's no snow. We're layered in coats, scarves, hats, and gloves, and Mrs. Malloy promises that when we're finished she's taking me and Suesetta to meet up with the other teams to get hot tea and sandwiches. The junior members of the Housewives' League are mentored and taught how to canvass and sign up new members. Suesetta and I are lucky. We have been paired with Mrs. Peck and Mrs. Malloy.

Mrs. Peck says, "We're so glad you girls have joined the junior league. Mrs. Malloy and I see a lot of potential in you. You young folks are being prepared to take the baton from us old folks and be the leaders of tomorrow."

Mrs. Malloy says, "Today, we are going to show you what leadership looks like. When you see something happening that you think is wrong, you do something good about it to make it right. That's what we're doing today. Do you understand, ladies?"

"Yes, ma'am," Suesetta and I say together. We laugh and do a pinkie swear because we answered at the same time.

We've been walking all morning in Paradise Valley, where most of the black-owned businesses, restaurants, and nightclubs are. We go house to house, talking to the woman of the home. Mrs. Malloy and Mrs. Peck are good at what they do. They take turns leading the conversation. Soon it will be our turn. I study them—how they introduce themselves, how they make eye contact. I notice how they don't go on talking about the League right away. First they ask the woman how she is, find out some of the things she enjoys doing. They do a whole lot of listening before they talk. And once they begin talking, they fill in each other's sentences. While one is handing out a coupon, the other is getting the membership form ready.

Already, seven women have signed up today. Only one person closed the door in our faces. And there was one house, the one we just left, that wouldn't answer the door even though we could see someone peeking around the curtain.

I watch Mrs. Malloy and Mrs. Peck and take it all in, wondering if Suesetta and I will be like the two of them when we get older.

We leave the blocks where all the houses are and walk along Saint Antoine Street, where the businesses are. The whole street is stacked with buildings that have signs advertising famous singers and jazz bands like Sarah Vaughan, Ella Fitzgerald, Cab Calloway, and Duke Ellington.

We pass a nightclub with a sign that says BILLY ECKSTINE,

THIS SATURDAY AT 7 P.M. Oh, how I wish I could go. Wish I could hear his voice in real life instead of just on spinning vinyl. But I know that will never happen. At least not till I'm older and can get into a place like that on my own.

We walk over to Black Bottom, where people are going about their day. As we make our way to the next block that we'll be canvassing, people wave, or nod and say hello. Mrs. Malloy says, "It's a shame all of these people are crowded into these blocks. The rent is too high and the space is too small."

"Indeed it is," Mrs. Peck says. "A lady contacted me just yesterday asking that I reach out to the Department of Public Works because they aren't coming here to shovel the snow off the streets as often as they do other parts of town."

And when she says *other* I know she means the white part of town. But Mrs. Peck and Mrs. Malloy talk in code, as if Suesetta and I don't know who they're talking about. I hear them sometimes, talking in the kitchen, when I am in my room. They wait until I close the door and they think I can't hear them. But I know how they talk and pray and sometimes cry about the way some white folks mistreat us.

How even though this is the North and it's not supposed to be like the South, it still has its hate, its prejudice, its inequality. Mrs. Malloy says Negro people came here to escape lynching and inhumane treatment. They came looking for better-paying jobs and peace of mind.

I think about this as we walk down the street on our way to the next block. How so many people came to Detroit to start their lives over, like me. They came searching, like me. And they found Adams Avenue and Saint Antoine Street. They found Negro teachers, doctors, dentists, and business owners. They found the smell of new paint for a grand opening, dinner specials being simmered, sautéed, baked, or fried. Found the glamour of a press and curl, a slender skirt, and crisp white gloves. Found the sound of soulful music echoing from churches, parlors, or someone's living room window.

But that's not all they found. I hear Mrs. Malloy say, "Negroes might not be hanging from trees here, but there is still sorrow and injustice."

Mrs. Peck nods like she does at church.

Mrs. Malloy keeps talking. "But despite it all, we must find the good and praise it."

"Yes, indeed," Mrs. Peck says.

They make it seem so easy, but for me, finding the good is sometimes hard and I worry that no matter how much good we find, there will always be more bad. I try not to have any negative thoughts about white people or fear how much worse it could get for Negroes. I try to focus on good things, I do. But I can't help but worry sometimes, and there's no telling Worry what to do. Worry is stubborn—she won't leave me alone.

We turn off the busy street onto a block where people live. The clouds shift and the sky fades to light gray. Mrs. Malloy pulls her shawl closer to her chest.

It's our turn to do the talking now. Suesetta goes first. We step onto the porch of the next house, ring the doorbell. A young woman comes to the door.

"Hello, ma'am, my name is Suesetta. I'm here today to gain your support and help make a difference in our community." Suesetta takes a breath and says, "We ask that you not buy where you can't be hired."

I can hear children in the background, one crying and the other screaming. The woman turns away from us, yells,

"Edward—give him back his choo choo train!" And then the crying stops. "I apologize," she says.

"Um, that's okay," Suesetta says. She looks at Mrs. Peck and Mrs. Malloy, who are standing behind us, close enough to help out if we need it but far enough to let us feel like we're doing this on our own.

We were taught to first ask the woman if we can come in, but before Suesetta says this part, Mrs. Malloy whispers, "It's okay, Suesetta. She's busy right now."

The woman asks us to come in anyway. "Oh, no, I'm a big supporter of the work you all are doing. Come on in, please," she says.

We step into her house and sit on the sofa. She tells her children to go to their room, and once they close the bedroom door, the house gets quieter.

"Thank you for stopping by. I was just telling my mother-in-law that I would like to become a member of the Housewives' League, and here you are."

"Who's your mother-in-law?" Mrs. Peck asks.

"Marietta Haines," the woman says. "Oh, and I'm Ruth." She shakes our hands.

"Well, it's nice to meet you, Ruth," Mrs. Malloy says. "I think I know Mrs. Haines. She joined us around a month ago. Lives about three blocks from here and goes to Mount Sinai Church, yes?"

"Yes, ma'am, she does," Mrs. Ruth says.

They talk a bit about Mrs. Haines and I'm sitting here thinking, *Who doesn't Mrs. Malloy know?* Mrs. Malloy gives Suesetta the look that says, *Go on with the pitch,* so Suesetta clears her throat and says, "Mrs. Ruth, we'd like to share some good news with you."

"Well, isn't this sweet," she says. "Go right ahead, please, you have my undivided attention." Mrs. Ruth smiles at Mrs. Malloy and sits down in a chair across from the sofa.

"Well," Suesetta says, "the Detroit Housewives' League has helped to create seventy thousand jobs for Negro men and women."

"Yes, and I am proud to say, young ladies, that my husband is one of the men hired after you all shut that meatpacking industry down."

Neither Suesetta nor I has any idea what she's talking about and I think she realizes this, so she tells us the story.

"In 1935, Negro housewives got together and boycotted the meatpacking industry because they refused to hire Negroes. The goal of the Housewives' League was to force the general stores in the city to hire colored folk. If the store owners thought our money was good enough to take for purchasing their products, then certainly our people were good enough to hire. Am I right?"

Suesetta and I both say, "Yes, ma'am."

She says, "It is the work of the Housewives' League that helped to get my husband hired. And it was a blessing to our family."

All day long we have been collecting stories from strangers telling us how much they appreciate Mrs. Peck, Mrs. Malloy, and the work of all the women in the Housewives' League. Suesetta says, "Ma'am, here is a membership form for you to complete." After Mrs. Ruth is finished filling out her form, we say our goodbyes. Her sons run out of their room chasing each other, the same one crying again because his brother won't share the choo choo train.

"We'll let you get back to your family," Mrs. Malloy says with a smile, glancing at the young boys as they whiz by.

When we step outside, Suesetta hands me the bundle of membership forms and coupons. "You're next," she says.

I'd known my turn was coming sooner or later, but going next makes me think twice about doing this. When we get to the next house, I ring the doorbell but no one answers, so we just leave a coupon and keep going. At the next home, a dog starts barking so loud when we approach the gate that all of us freeze. He runs back and forth, growling at us.

Mrs. Peck says, "Let's go to the next block, ladies."

And I'm relieved because Phyllis lives on the next block, right on the corner. She might not think the Housewives' League is any fun, but she's not going to shut the door in *my* face.

I knock and it takes a while, but finally the door opens. "Hi, Phyllis!"

"Hi, Betty." Phyllis looks at me, then looks past me and sees I'm not alone. She says hello to everyone.

"Is your momma home?" I ask.

"Um, well, she might be busy," Phyllis says.

"We won't be long. Just want to give her a coupon."

Phyllis lets us in and disappears for a moment, then comes back. "She's coming," she tells us. We sit in her living room and wait for her mother to join us. There is one small sofa against the windowsill. On both sides of the sofa, there are armchairs draped in throw blankets and a worn coffee table is in the middle. I can smell dinner cooking and realize we've been out canvassing all day and I'm getting hungry.

"Are we getting together after church tomorrow?" Phyllis asks, looking at Suesetta.

"Only if you bring your Billy Eckstine record again," Suesetta says. "And we can listen to the new one my momma bought me—Duke Ellington."

Just then, Mrs. Boyd walks in. She takes one look at Mrs. Malloy, then looks at Phyllis with her hand on her hip. "I've told you about letting people in without getting my permission, child."

"But it's Mrs. Malloy and Mrs. Peck."

"Hi, Helen. Hello, Fannie," Mrs. Boyd says. "With all due respect, I've told you on several occasions that I am not interested in your highfalutin boycott or whatever fancy pamphlet you're pushing this time."

"Now, Mrs. Boyd, let the girls have their say," Mrs. Peck says with a smile but irritation in her voice.

Mrs. Boyd looks at me. "Yes, dear, I know. You don't want me to buy where folk that look like me can't work, right? Well, guess what—Sears has a sale going on right now. So unless you all are prepared to buy my daughter a warm coat she can wear for the rest of winter, Fannie, Helen, I suggest you leave. Boycotting big department stores is not going to change anything."

Mrs. Malloy and Mrs. Peck don't move, so Suesetta and I sit still, too. Mrs. Malloy clears her throat. "Mrs. Boyd, now listen—"

"No, Helen, you listen. I give you two all the respect when we're in the Lord's house, but this is *my* house. It might not be as fancy as yours, but it's what the Lord done give me, and I am not interested in none of your foolishness. I have dinner to make for my family right now." She stands at the door and opens it.

Mrs. Malloy stands, takes a coupon gently out of my hands, and leaves it on the coffee table. "In case you change your mind," she says, and motions us along.

We leave.

I look back at the house before we walk away. Phyllis is standing at the window, looking at me with a rainstorm in her eyes. I get the feeling she won't be bringing her records over after church tomorrow.

Fourteen

SPRING BLESSINGS:

My brown skin and the warmth it feels when the sun kisses it.

My eyes for seeing the blooming purple flowers coming back to say hello after being gone all winter long.

My ears for taking in the soul of Paradise Valley, the high heels clicking against pavement, pianos being tuned, kind, courteous voices mingling, "Hello, little lady."

My hands that can hold needle and thread and create something beautiful. My hand that knows how to shake another hand, firm and confident.

My voice that knows how to say my name with pride when looking directly into someone's eyes.

My head held high, my shoulders back, my feet that glide block after block, on a mission, with a purpose.

Fifteen

APRIL SHOWERS HAVEN'T COME YET. IT'S warmer than usual and Mr. Malloy says this means it's going to be a hot summer. Suesetta, Phyllis, and I are walking home from school—they're going to their homes, but I'm going to work a few hours at the shoe repair store. I only have one more block to walk with them before I have to turn and go a different way. Before we split up I say, "My birthday is next month, May twenty-eighth. Mrs. Malloy said I could have a sleepover. Want to come?" I was never able to have friends spend the night when I lived with Ollie Mae. The house was for family, she always said. And besides, I never knew when she was going to lose her temper, and I didn't want Suesetta or Phyllis to ever witness that.

Suesetta is the first to say yes. "We can bake a cake in-stead of cookies and I'll borrow Kay's new red nail polish and we can do our nails and have our own Rose-Meta House of Beauty!"

Phyllis doesn't say anything.

Suesetta gives her a look, says, "You're coming, right?"

Phyllis shrugs. "I might be busy."

"Well, we don't have to do it on my actual birthday—"

"I just don't know, Betty. You know my mom doesn't really like me spending the night at other people's houses."

"Well, maybe she'll let you just this once since it's my birthday," I say.

"Maybe," Phyllis says.

"Well, ask her," I say. "It wouldn't be the same without you. You have to be there."

We reach the end of the block. I hug Suesetta and Phyllis like I always do when we say goodbye, but Phyllis doesn't hold on as tight as she normally does. I walk the rest of the way to the store wondering if Phyllis is mad at me, if I did something wrong. When I arrive, Mr. Malloy is just finishing up with a customer.

"Good afternoon, Betty. How was school?"

"It was good," I say. I don't tell him that Phyllis was acting strange, that things have been different ever since Suesetta and I went over to her house with Mrs. Malloy and Mrs. Peck.

I read my chore list and get right to work. Most days I work at the store, I sweep, dust, and wipe off the mirrors and counters. I was hoping to work the register, but Mr. Malloy says that's a big responsibility, that when I'm ready for it he'll teach me.

Seems like no matter how much I clean the floor, there is always dust to get rid of. When I'm not sweeping, I am arranging the shelves and restocking them with shoe polish, shoelaces, and shoe cushions. There are all kinds of dyes, polishes, and swatches of leather Mr. Malloy uses to restore the customers' shoes, handbags, wallets, and belts. He makes everything look brand-new. I line the bottles up real neat to make sure customers see them.

It's a slow, quiet afternoon until Phyllis's dad walks in carrying a pair of brown lace-up dress shoes. I'm hoping Phyllis is trailing behind him, that she came to apologize or explain herself, but then the door closes and I know that he came alone. "Hi, Lorenzo. Can you widen these for me?" Deacon Boyd asks.

Mr. Malloy looks the shoes over, then looks at Deacon Boyd's feet. "When do you need them back?"

"Three days. Can you get 'em back to me in three days?"

"That I can do," Mr. Malloy says. He begins to fill out an order form.

"Are you attending the prayer meeting tonight?" Deacon Boyd asks. "Heard Thurgood Marshall is going to be at Bethel."

"Yes, I heard. I don't know if I want to hear the rhetoric tonight," Mr. Malloy says. "I know he's trying to convince us that 'separate but equal' isn't enough but—"

"You think it is?"

"Well, I'm not too sure that desegregating schools is going to fix the Negro's problem."

"Now, come on here, Lorenzo Malloy—"

Mr. Malloy waves his hands. "Let me finish, let me finish." He signs the order form and hands it to Deacon Boyd.

"Now, if Thurgood Marshall or anyone else is talking about instituting policies where we Negro men can really exercise our full rights as men and participate in the policing, educating, and housing of our own families and neighborhoods equal to any, I'd be front row for that." Mr. Malloy looks at me and points to a box sitting in the corner. "Betty, those items need to be stocked," he tells me, and I know this is his way of getting me out of the front room and into the back storage area.

As soon as I am in the other room, he keeps talking.

"I'm not sure what desegregated schools are going to do for the Negro man. Let's think about this—what will happen to Negro teachers? What will happen to our children who will be sitting next to white children for the first time with no one preparing them? Why isn't anyone talking about white children integrating into Negro schools? It's imposing the notion that we are inferior, and by having our children travel across town, it's imposing the notion that white schools are superior," Mr. Malloy says.

"You think so?"

"I know so. You think those white teachers are going to

teach *all* children the truth about what the Negro has contributed to this country?" Mr. Malloy asks. "I'm not saying something shouldn't be done, I'm just not sure desegregation is a thought-out answer. You see what Mrs. Peck and my wife are doing? That's a thought-out response. Getting colored people to realize just how much spending power we have, fighting for the advancement of the economic status of colored people—now, *that's* where real change for the Negro man will happen. We have to show everybody the power of our dollar because that's what matters to the white man the most. This dollar."

Deacon Boyd laughs. "This coming from a Negro who runs his own business. Of course you want *us* to be your patrons."

"Look here now, I may have graduated from Tuskegee, but I'm an ole country man from Arkansas. I grew up in the very same circumstances of every other colored man in this country, and I refused to let anything stop me from exercising my rights as a man, a husband, a father, and a businessman."

"Hmm. If it could only be that easy—"

"What are you talking about, easy? I'm here by the grace of God. Nothing about starting a business as a Negro man during the Depression, mass lynchings, and the Jim Crow laws was easy," Mr. Malloy says. "Not to mention keeping this business thriving for my wife and my daughter."

I can't help but smile when he calls me his daughter. The word echoes in my ears, sounding better than my favorite song. I want to run out and hug him, tell him how grateful I am, tell him how much I love being *his daughter*. But instead, I just keep unloading boxes, keep doing my job, keep listening to Mr. Malloy talk and talk. He likes to debate with his customers. They must like it, too. Sometimes, men come in here and they don't even want their shoes fixed, they don't even buy anything. They just stop by on their lunch break or after work to talk with Mr. Malloy. Lots of times they debate about the Detroit Tigers— who's the best player and whatnot. But when they really get going, really start talking about things that matter, Mr. Malloy sends me to the storeroom. Guess he doesn't realize that I hear them anyway.

They keep on going until Deacon Boyd says, "Well, I think that's about all the sparring I have in me for today, Lorenzo, sir." He is laughing and Mr. Malloy is laughing, too. "We'll have to continue next time."

"Yes sir, until the next time," Mr. Malloy says.

I hear the bell clink when Deacon Boyd leaves, so I know it's safe for me to come back out. I go back to dusting and arranging the shoe polish on the shelf.

The bell announces that another customer has entered. It's Mrs. Malloy. She comes in carrying a box of flyers in her arms. "Hot off the press," she says. "We're going to hand these out at grocery stores that are still refusing to hire us." She sets them on the counter. Mr. Malloy kisses her on her cheek. She kisses me on mine.

Mr. Malloy holds up one of the flyers. The top says SELECTIVE BUYING CAMPAIGN and there are two lists. On the left is a list of businesses that trade with and hire Negroes, and on the right is a list of stores to boycott. "Oh, I see you added lists of stores. That's good. Yes, that's good."

"Mrs. Peck's idea," Mrs. Malloy says. She takes the

flyer and puts it back in the box. "How much longer will you be?" she asks.

"Not long at all," Mr. Malloy says.

He closes up the store and we ride home. On the way, it starts to rain. Not a storm, but enough to have the wipers on. They slide from side to side, erasing raindrops. We drive past Bethel and I can't even believe how many people are standing outside waiting to get in. The line twists and turns around the corner. People are sharing umbrellas and a few people are standing under wet newspapers.

"That Thurgood Marshall sure does draw a crowd," Mr. Malloy says.

"Oh, yes, he does. And we need to get every single body that's out there right now to come volunteer at the Dunbar Community Center," Mrs. Malloy says. "Help is needed in the baby clinic, and they could also use some tutors. Betty, can you remind me to include it in the announcements at our next Housewives' meeting?"

"Yes, ma'am."

I lean forward in my seat, making sure they can hear

me. "But he isn't just going to speak, is he? This is a prayer meeting, too, right?"

I really want to see Thurgood Marshall—in real life, not just newspapers—but Mr. Malloy keeps driving, right past the church and toward our house.

Mrs. Malloy turns to me and says, "Yes, there will be praying, Betty. But hard work is equally important. Bible says, 'Faith without works is dead.'"

Sixteen

THE WEEKEND GOES BY FAST AND IS MOSTLY full of homework and volunteer work with Mrs. Malloy. It is Monday and the walk home from school was lonely because Suesetta is sick and Phyllis's mom picked her up. Even though I just saw Shirley, Jimmie, and Juanita yesterday at church, they are taking turns on the phone telling me how much they miss me. I talk with Shirley last. She barely says hello before asking, "When are you coming back home, Betty?"

"I live here with the Malloys now."

"But why? Why can't you just visit the Malloys and live here with us?"

I think Shirley is crying but I'm not sure. I don't know how to answer her question. I could just tell her the truth—tell her I'm not coming home because Ollie Mae doesn't love me the way she loves them. But instead, I say, "I'm not sure when I'm coming back," as if I plan on returning. I tell her, "We'll see each other at church next Sunday." And that part is true, so I don't feel too much like a fibber.

"But Sunday is a long ways away," Shirley says.

"Maybe the week will go by fast," I tell Shirley.

I hear Ollie Mae calling Shirley, then Shirley says into the phone, "Betty, Momma wants to talk with you."

Ollie Mae gets on the line. "Hello?"

"Hi, Ollie Mae."

"Is everything okay? Sounds like you have a cold," she says.

"Everything is fine," I say even though my throat is hurting just a little. How did she know?

It is quiet for a while and I think I hear Arthur listening to the radio and the boys' footsteps as they're running around.

Ollie Mae clears her throat. "You know, you might

want to tell Mrs. Malloy to put some honey, lemon, and eucalyptus oil in a jar. That will help your achy throat."

"Okay, Ollie Mae, I will tell her."

"And tell her to keep some Vernor's Ginger Soda in the house. Tell her to warm it and put a little lemon in it if you get a bellyache, okay?"

"Yes, ma'am."

Silence.

"And tea. Make sure you drink plenty of dandelion root tea," she says.

"I will."

"Good, good. Well, okay. I guess I should get going."

"Okay," I say. "Bye."

"Bye."

When I hang up the phone, all I can think about is how much I miss my sisters, how much I miss sitting around the dining room table together. I wish they could come spend the night here with me every now and then.

The doorbell rings. I look out the window and see Kay standing on the porch. I let her in. "Hi, Betty. I hope I didn't interrupt dinner," she says.

"It's okay. I'm just here doing homework. Mr. Malloy is still at work and Mrs. Malloy is at a meeting."

"My mother sent me over to ask Mrs. Malloy if she has any butter."

I'm sure Mrs. Malloy wouldn't mind, so I tell Kay to have a seat while I get it for her.

She follows me to the kitchen and sits at the table. I go to the icebox. Kay says, "So, um, what are you all doing for Easter?"

"I—hmm, I don't know. Dinner, I guess."

"You guess?"

"Well, we'll go to church, of course, but I don't know what we'll do afterward. Arthur always took us to church for the Easter egg hunt every year. Maybe I'll still go, maybe I've outgrown it. Not sure," I say.

The butter is cut but we keep talking. Kay asks me, "So, how does it feel to have two mothers?"

I have never thought about it this way—that I have two mothers. I shrug. "Ollie Mae has never been a *real* mother to me."

"Well, at least you know her. You get to hear her voice.

You're able to look at her and see what parts of you come from her," Kay says.

"What do you mean? You see your mom everyday."

"Yes, but my mom and dad aren't my birth parents. They adopted me when I was a baby."

"Really? So, Aunt Nina and Uncle Clyde aren't your *real* parents?"

"They are my *real* parents—their love is real, everything about our relationship is real," Kay says. "My biological father was never in the picture. My biological mother died during labor. But the truth is, Nina is my real mom and Clyde is my real dad. Doesn't matter that I was born to someone else. They don't really make a big deal about it."

Even though it's just the two of us in this big house, I lower my voice, lean forward, and say, "But it *is* a big deal, don't you think?"

"I guess." Kay nods. "Love is always a big deal."

Seventeen

MAY'S BLESSINGS:

I am counting my blessings tonight and thinking about Kay and how she never got to hear her mother's voice. I am counting my blessings tonight and thinking about all the ways love is a big deal, how it is the honey, lemon, and eucalyptus oil that Ollie Mae makes for a scratchy throat. The extra dollar Mr. Malloy gives me, telling me how hardworking I am. Love is talking to your sister on the telephone and running out of words to say but staying on the line anyway. Love is not letting a friend stop being your friend for no good reason at all. Love is family being who you choose and who chooses you.

Eighteen

I CAN'T WAIT FOR SUESETTA TO COME OVER. She's going to help me set up for the biscuits-and-tea gathering Mrs. Malloy is hosting for the leaders of the House-wives' League. Once the tea is over, Suesetta will spend the night and we'll celebrate my birthday. Phyllis's mom said she couldn't come over, but Suesetta and I will call her later so she can be a part of at least some of my birthday.

Just as I am slicing the lemon cake Mrs. Malloy baked, the phone rings. "Betty, it's for you," Mrs. Malloy says.

I take the phone hoping it's Phyllis saying that her mother changed her mind, but as I say hello, I hear a choir of voices singing, "Happy birthday to you, happy birthday to you. Happy birthday dear Betty, happy birthday to you!"

Shirley, Jimmie, Juanita, Sonny, and Henry are singing to me. Arthur and Ollie Mae, too. At the end of the song all the girls start talking at once. "Okay, okay," Ollie Mae says. "One at a time."

Shirley goes first. "Betty, did you have your cake and ice cream yet?"

"Yeah," Jimmie blurts out. "Did you get to have as much as you wanted, like we do for our birthdays?"

"Not yet," I tell them. I don't even know if Mrs. Malloy would let me have all the ice cream I could eat. It's not something most adults let kids do, but Ollie Mae always said that when it's your birthday, you should get to have as much ice cream as you want, and she'd let us pick our own flavor. Mine is always butter pecan. "I'll definitely have some later," I say.

"Well, what are you doing for your birthday?" Shirley asks.

"Suesetta's spending the night."

"Oh." Shirley sighs and it sounds like a wind of sadness just rushed through the phone.

I hear Ollie Mae say, "All right girls, let Betty get back to what she was doing." Then her voice sounds much closer. "Betty?"

"Yes, ma'am?"

"We're going to go now, but the girls, uh, really wanted to call. We . . . we all wanted to call," she says. "Happy birthday."

"Thank you," I say.

When I hang up the phone I stand for a moment, holding on to the sound of all those voices singing to me. So many good smells are floating through the house—cinnamon scones, lemon pound cake, chocolate cake. Mrs. Malloy has also baked oatmeal cookies and shortbread cookies. I think maybe this might be the best birthday ever.

Once Suesetta comes over, Mrs. Malloy says, "I'm going to teach you how to make lavender lemonade." She sets the ingredients out on the counter: lemons, raw honey, and dried lavender. She tells Suesetta, "Now, I want you to measure eight cups of water and a half cup of manuka honey, and let's get that pot on the stove." Then she takes a small bag of lemons, cuts each one in half, and hands the halves over to me. "You'll work on the lemonade," she says. "Start squeezing these."

Once I'm finished squeezing lemons, I pour the juice into two pitchers that are half full of cold water. Suesetta strains the lavender out of the boiling water. Now that the lavender has been simmering, the whole house smells like spring.

"Okay, it's time to combine everything," Mrs. Malloy says. Suesetta pours her concoction into both pitchers. We each get to sample it just before she puts it in the refrigerator to chill. It's the best lemonade I've ever tasted.

"Now, let's get the buffet set up." Mrs. Malloy hands us silver serving trays and white china. We set the desserts and beverages on the dining room table with the crystal glasses. Mr. Malloy has taken the white wooden chairs from the basement into the living room to make sure everyone has a seat. Fresh bouquets of lavender and white roses are in the living room and the dining room.

"Ladies, we sure know how to host a tea," Mrs. Malloy says.

"We sure do," I say. I step back and take a look at everything. "It's perfect."

We rush to get dressed before our guests arrive, and

once everyone shows up, Suesetta and I blend into the wallpaper. We don't say anything, just take it all in. We're the youngest girls in the junior league. Kay and three other girls are here, too, but two are sixteen and the other is seventeen.

Before the official meeting begins, the women eat and sip tea, and catch each other up on the community happenings. Mrs. Malloy starts the meeting. "Good afternoon, ladies. As you know, Mrs. Peck is not aware of this meeting today because we have secretly gathered here to finish planning her appreciation service. All of the Housewives' League chapters from around the nation will join us next month to celebrate the accomplishments of the League and honor our fearless leader."

The women respond with smiles, little claps, and nods. Then Mrs. Malloy tells everyone the date of the event and says, "This date was selected because Paul Robeson will also be in town campaigning and he's agreed to come to Bethel, ladies, and bless us with his wisdom and a song," she says.

"Sing?" a woman shouts. "He doesn't need to sing a note so long as I see that handsome face, yes, Lord."

Suesetta and I look at each other and bust out laughing. We put our hands on our faces, covering our mouths so Mrs. Malloy doesn't see us and send us upstairs.

I don't know who this Paul Robeson is, but every time his name comes up, women start blushing. He must be a really good speaker, the way he makes smiles appear on all the ladies' faces.

Mrs. Malloy says, "Now, ladies, let's focus. I only bring him up because I think we should meet with him and talk about the work we're doing. We need him to lend his voice to our cause. He's world-renowned, and if we are smart, we will get him to use his national platform to shed light on what we're doing right here in Detroit."

One of the women adds, "It's a wonder he's making the time to visit with us, with all the advocating he's doing with President Truman to put an end to the lynching of people all over the South. Doesn't look like it's working, but at least he's trying."

The woman sitting next to her shakes her head, says, "How in the world is Truman going to say he upholds the Constitution when he won't pass legislation to end lynching?"

"And to think," another Housewife adds, "the Negro has traveled far away from his family and laid down his life in a war for this country only to return back to a system of laws that still allows him to be tied up helpless and hung from a tree while people just stand around watching the life go out of him. I will never understand this kind of hatred and barbarism. Lord help me, I won't."

Mrs. Malloy picks up a lemon-ginger cookie from the plate in the middle of the table. She bites into the cookie, wipes the fallen crumbs from her lap, and says, "By not doing anything, Truman is telling all of us—Negroes and whites—that it's perfectly fine to murder a Negro in this country and get away with it."

One of the women adds, "Some of those folks will kill their own kind if they stand for justice. Can you believe that?"

I think maybe Mrs. Malloy forgot that Suesetta and I are in the room, because as soon as she looks over at us, she says, "Oh, girls, you can excuse yourselves now." But then as we walk away, she adds, "But one more thing—I'd like the two of you to introduce Mrs. Peck at the event."

"In front of everyone?" I ask.

"Yes—you'll talk about the League and the work Mrs. Peck has done and what she means to you." She says it like it's not a big deal, what she's asking us to do. "We'll talk more later," she says. This, I know, is her way of telling us to go to my room, close the door, and let the grown folk be. Except everyone here isn't grown—Kay and her three friends are here, nodding and snacking, and fitting right in with all of the adults. I am nowhere close to being Kay's age. But once I am older, I plan to sit in on all the conversations, tell everyone how I feel.

Suesetta plops down on my bed. "What do you want to do?" I ask.

"We can paint our nails," Suesetta says. She goes into her overnight bag and pulls out the red nail polish Kay let us borrow.

Once we paint our nails, there isn't much more we can do for a while. We just sit and wait, and blow on our fingers, and shake our wrists, and wait some more. This goes on for about an hour. Mine dry faster because I didn't use as much as Suesetta, who has put such a thick coat on, it will take all night for hers to dry.

"We could call Phyllis now," I say. I pick up the phone and dial. The phone rings twice.

"Hello?" It's Mrs. Boyd.

"Hello, may I speak with Phyllis?"

"Who's calling?"

"This is Betty—and Suesetta," I tell her.

"Betty, Phyllis is busy doing chores right now. I'll let her know you called."

"Oh, okay, thank—"

Mrs. Boyd hangs up before I can even finish my sentence.

I tell Suesetta, "Next time, you should call. I think Mrs. Boyd likes you better."

Suesetta says. "You should call back and tell her you're Loretta. She'll let Phyllis talk to Loretta." Suesetta is sure of this. Loretta is in our sewing class. She used to go to Bethel, too, but then her father became the pastor of his own church, so we don't see her on Sundays anymore.

"I can't do that," I tell her. "She already heard my voice!"

Suesetta thinks for a moment. "I'll do it," she says. I dial for her and then hand her the receiver. It must ring longer than two times because it takes a while for Suesetta to say, "Hi, may I speak to Phyllis?" Then, "This is Loretta." Suesetta is talking higher than normal, mimicking Loretta's birdlike voice. "Yes, ma'am, Loretta," she repeats. Her eyes get big but then look at ease as she says, "Yes, ma'am, I can hold." Suesetta smiles at me and motions to me to come to the phone. I stand real close to her, leaning my head toward the receiver so I can hear Phyllis, but I make sure not to touch Suesetta's nails.

Phyllis says, "Loretta?" all confused.

"No, Phyllis, it's me, Suesetta." She holds the phone closer to me.

"And Betty, too," I call out.

"Oh," Phyllis says, like she's not happy it's us. "I can't talk right now," she tells us.

"Well, then, why'd your mom give you the phone?" I ask.

She doesn't answer.

"Look, Betty, I can't be your friend anymore. My mom doesn't want me hanging out with you and Suesetta."

I don't mean to snatch the phone, but I can't help myself. "What do you mean? Why?"

"Do I really need to tell you?" Phyllis asks.

"Is it because we're in the Housewives' League?" I ask.

Suesetta calls out, "We can still be friends even though your mom doesn't agree with Mrs. Peck and Mrs. Malloy." Her voice sounds hopeful, but her face is sad.

"It's not about my mother disagreeing with them. *I* disagree with them. With all of you," she says. "I don't want to be friends with girls who believe that buying expensive products from Negro stores is going to change anything. A tube of Dudley's hair cream isn't going to bring any of the people back to life who are strung up on trees."

I look at Suesetta. Both of us are so confused and already missing our friend. Phyllis keeps talking. "You two are so boring. We don't have fun anymore," she says. Then, without even giving us a chance to respond, she says, "I have to go. Bye."

Suesetta and I retell the whole conversation to each other, like we need to hear it again in order to understand what just happened. Finally, she says, "We have to do something else. We can't just mope around all night. Wanna play a game?"

I can't think of anything except all the hurtful things Phyllis said.

Suesetta says, "How about Truth, Dare, Double Dare, Promise, or Repeat? You first."

"Double dare," I say.

"I double dare you to pick up the phone and dial a random number and have a conversation with whoever answers, like you know them."

"Just a random person?" I ask.

"Yes. And then I'll do a dare," Suesetta says.

I hesitate, then pick up the phone. I dial the first random numbers that come to my mind. An elderly man answers the phone. His voice is feeble and low. "Hello?"

I put on the most adult-sounding, sophisticated voice I can fake. "Hello?"

"Who's calling?" the old man asks.

"Me," I say.

"Me, who?" the old man asks.

"Who, me?" I say.

Suesetta starts laughing—so loud that the old man hears her.

"You kids stop tying up my line with your silly games!" the old man yells. He hangs up.

We burst into laughter. And even though it's Suesetta's turn, I make another call. Who would have thought calling strangers would be more fun than calling Phyllis? The second call ends with even more laughter.

"What are you girls doing in there?" Mrs. Malloy asks.

I don't know why the question gets us laughing even more. "Nothing," we say in unison.

Mrs. Malloy is not one to be fooled. She opens the door. "I could use some help with cleaning up," she says.

We help get the house back to looking like our house.

Later that night, when Suesetta and I are lying in bed falling asleep, I say to Suesetta, "One more round?"

"Okay," she says.

"You pick. Truth, Dare, Double Dare, Promise, or Repeat?"

"Promise," Suesetta says.

"Promise me we'll be friends forever?"

Nineteen

I GO TO SLEEP COUNTING AND COUNTING:

I am thankful for family and friends. I am thankful for the way laughter swells up mighty like the ocean, then settles like soft waves and comes again.

I am thankful for surprise phone calls and birthday wishes.

I am thankful for the look in Suesetta's eyes when she calls me her best friend, how I know she means it when she says it again and again: "Forever."

Twenty

THE NEXT FEW WEEKS WE STAY BUSY
planning Mrs. Peck's appreciation service. It's been hard to
organize everything without her knowing, but now the day
has almost come, so we can stop whispering after church
and having private meetings without her. The event is happening tomorrow after our regular Sunday morning service. Today, Suesetta and I are practicing our speech and
trying on clothes. Suesetta walks over to her closet. "What
should I wear tomorrow?" she asks.

I look through the hanging clothes—mostly dresses—
and pick out the ones I think are fancy enough for the service but not too fancy. I lay them on her bed. "These are
cute," I tell her.

Suesetta looks them over, then sighs. She goes back to her closet and pulls out three more. "Okay, out of all of these, which one?" she asks.

I point to the yellow dress.

"Pick two more."

I point to a light-blue dress with red flowers and the pleated navy-blue one trimmed with ivory ribbon around the edges.

"Okay, so out of these three, which one?"

"I still like the yellow one the best," I tell her. "I love the color and I like how it fits you on the top and bellows out on the bottom."

Suesetta holds the light-blue dress up to her. "Are you sure?"

"Yes—it's really pretty."

"Okay. I just want to make sure. I mean, this is a big deal. People are coming from Cleveland, Toledo, Chicago, Pittsburgh. And don't forget, Paul Robeson will be here, too."

All of a sudden my heart is pounding. I know it's a big deal, but hearing it again is making me feel like I am going to be speaking in front of the whole world. "Aren't you nervous?" I ask.

Suesetta assures me, "It's just like having to say our Christmas speeches in front of the congregation, only we don't have to memorize it, so it's even better. You're good at speaking anyway, Betty." Suesetta looks over the light-blue dress with red flowers again. "I think I'll wear this one," she says. "What do you think?"

I think she's not listening to what I think, so I tell her, "Why don't you do eeny, meeny, miny, mo?"

Suesetta starts singing the song, pointing to the dresses spread across her bed. The light-blue dress is out first. "Aw, but I like that one," Suesetta says.

I laugh. I know there will be many more rounds.

Twenty-One

JUST LIKE MRS. MALLOY PROMISED, PAUL
Robeson is at our church this morning. While Pastor
Dames introduces him, Paul Robeson sits like a tender giant,
strong and confident.

"He didn't have to come to Bethel and bless us, Church
family," Pastor Dames says. "Yes, he is a famous actor. Yes,
he is a world-class singer. But this man is so much more.
Mr. Robeson stands tall all around the world in the struggle
for us colored folk. Brothers and sisters," he says, "it is an
honor to have him with us on this Sunday morning. Please,
let us stand and welcome our mighty brother to Bethel
AME, Mr. Paul Robeson!"

The whole congregation stands. We clap and cheer him on. Mr. Robeson can barely say a word because everyone is clapping and cheering him on. Especially all of the women.

He takes the microphone, grips it in his big hands. I hear thunder in his throat when he speaks. It shakes me on the inside. Every person in the church is still. His voice reminds me of the days with my Aunt Fannie Mae, of the towering trees and Georgia's glistening stars, of the rooster that woke us to the morning sun.

When he talks, he speaks about power and peace, and he gets the church all excited. "As an American citizen, I speak against injustice. I will always speak for peace. No one can silence me. Because the Lord is on the side of the righteous, and I am on the side of the Lord."

"Amen, brother!" men shout.

Then Paul Robeson sings "Amazing Grace."

Through many dangers, toils, and snares,
I have already come;

'Tis Grace hath brought me safe thus far,
And Grace will lead me home.

After he sings, it's time for me and Suesetta to introduce Mrs. Peck. I can hardly feel my feet as we walk to the front of the sanctuary. Once we're at the podium, Suesetta grabs my hand and gives it a quick squeeze. My nerves settle a bit and everything I'm supposed to say just flows right out.

I read Mrs. Peck's biography first. It's mostly just stating her birthday, the year she started the Housewives' League, and how, as a woman, she is a leader of the church. I feel so proud as I recite the part I wrote all by myself. I fold my paper and make sure my voice is going into the microphone. "What I admire the most about Mrs. Peck is her strength and determination. I've spent time canvassing neighborhoods with her to get as many women as possible to sign up, and it requires a lot of hard work. Mrs. Peck takes the time to teach us girls so we can make sure everybody understands that Negroes are human beings, too. And as human beings we have feelings and we have power."

Suesetta says the next part. "Sometimes people don't

even open their doors because they are scared and don't know that they have the power and the right to make change. So, for Mrs. Peck to have started this organization with no guarantee that people would support her or that white business owners would change their minds and agree with her, I think that's a testament to her faith and determination."

The congregation claps and a few people say amen.

Then I say the last part. The part I was most nervous about sharing. I pause for a moment, thinking maybe I should just end it there, but then Suesetta nudges me and the words just come right out like they needed the push. "What I like most about Mrs. Peck is her resilience. I know what it's like to have someone you love more than anything in the world die and go to heaven. I know that emptiness hurts so much, but Mrs. Peck keeps her joy. She teaches us not to wallow in any misery, but to grow from it." Then I turn to Mrs. Peck and look her in her eyes. "Mrs. Peck, your leadership is an example to all of us girls, and even the boys," I say. "Thank you."

Mrs. Peck is wiping her eyes with a white handkerchief.

Suesetta says, "On behalf of the African Methodist Episcopal Church at Bethel, we thank you for being a role model to us and a pillar of hope to the nation."

Then Suesetta steps closer to the mic and says, "Ladies and gentlemen, please join us in welcoming our faithful leader, Mrs. Fannie B. Peck." She says it perfectly, just as we practiced it.

The church is full of applause, and every single person is standing.

I know people are mostly clapping for Mrs. Peck, but it feels good standing in front of everyone, having them smile and cheer us on, listening to our every word. It feels like family here.

Once Mrs. Peck comes to the microphone, Suesetta and I take our turns to hug her and then we walk back to the second row and take our seats. "Thank you, thank you," Mrs. Peck says. "What this means, you'll never know." Mrs. Peck thanks a long list of people—some who aren't even here, but she says their names anyway. Then she says, "I want to remind everyone that the House-wives' League is more than a trade campaign. The

Housewives' League is about investing in ourselves and in our children. It's about supporting our men and believing that we have, within our own community, everything we need."

People clap.

"This is about power. The color green has power. Yes, Church. Money has power. The Bible says, 'Where your heart is, there will your treasure be.' So I ask you today, do you love yourselves?"

"Yes!" people shout.

"Do you love your families? Your community?"

"Amen," people shout.

"Well, if you do, it is time to show it by how you spend your money. Don't buy where we can't work! Invest in your own communities first."

Most people stand and clap when Mrs. Peck says this.

But not Phyllis's mom. Not Ollie Mae.

"I pray you continue the work," Mrs. Peck says. "I pray you continue to believe in the power of *us*. It is the only way we can accomplish any goal—by coming together. Thank you."

Mrs. Peck is escorted back to her seat. The audience gives her another standing ovation.

❧

After service, the adults linger, talking while we play and run around until Deacon Boyd tells us to stop playing in the Lord's house. He has us walk through the pews and pick up any left-behind programs, or tissues, or anything that should be thrown away. A small group of us begins cleaning while most of the kids continue to run around like they didn't even hear him.

I am in one aisle, Kay is in the next. I bend over and pick up a fan, a bulletin. By the time we walk through each pew, most people have gone. Ollie Mae hasn't left yet. She is sitting in a pew, waiting for Arthur to finish up his conversation with Deacon Boyd. That means my sisters and brothers are probably off somewhere playing tag, even though Deacon Boyd has fussed at them at least three times now.

Mrs. Malloy is deep in conversation with one of the

members from Chicago. They have been talking in the corner this whole time. One of the ushers, Mrs. White, comes over to me carrying a black leather purse. "You were excellent, young lady."

"Thank you," I say.

"Do you know to whom this belongs?" she asks.

"No, ma'am."

"Hmm," she says. She scans the sanctuary. "Well, it can't belong to any of you young folk. Ollie Mae, is this yours?" She holds the purse up.

Ollie Mae shakes her head.

She asks another woman, "Is this yours?"

"Not mine," the woman says.

"Excuse me, Mrs. Malloy—" she calls out. But Mrs. Malloy doesn't answer. All of her attention is on the woman from Chicago. "Mrs. Malloy?" Mrs. White raises her voice just a bit.

Mrs. Malloy doesn't hear her.

"Well, it's got to be one of theirs," Mrs. White says. "At least I hope it is."

Mr. Malloy walks into the sanctuary, coming from

downstairs. Mrs. White looks at him, says, "Mr. Malloy, is this your wife's purse?"

He looks it over. "I can't say. Doesn't look like it. Then again, they all look the same to me." He laughs.

Mrs. White laughs, too.

Mr. Malloy calls out, "Helen—Helen?"

Nothing.

No one can get her attention.

I don't know what comes over me. I guess I just want to help. I don't know. But for some reason, I open my mouth and shout in my loudest voice, "Mother! Is this your purse?" I didn't expect to say *Mother*. The word slipped off my tongue like I had said it before. I didn't even know it was ever there.

I walk over to Mrs. Malloy so I can give her the purse. As I walk across the sanctuary, it's like my feet are in quicksand. I see everyone all at once. Suesetta stops in the middle of the choir stand—where the altos usually are— holding a hymnal in her arms. The ushers look down at the floor. Mr. Malloy is rubbing his balding head. The woman from Chicago has a smile on her face. She reaches out her hand. "Oh, thank you, sweetheart, it's mine," she says.

She says this just as I walk past the pew that Ollie Mae is sitting in. I do not look at Ollie Mae. I just keep walking. Not because I don't care about her, but because I think hearing your child call another woman *Mother* might be hurtful. It was not my intention to hurt her, but I can't take back what I just said, so I just keep walking, right past her pew. I hand the purse to the woman from Chicago. She reaches into it and pulls out a butterscotch candy. "Thank you, baby," she says.

"You're welcome," I tell her. I take the candy and now I am closer to Mrs. Malloy. She is standing there looking at me with joy all over her face. She hugs me. By the time I turn around, Ollie Mae is gone. Shirley, Juanita, Jimmie, and the boys, too.

❧

That night I lie in bed mouthing the word *Mother* over and over.

My lips are not used to saying this word. The last time I said *Mother*, I wasn't even two years old, probably just forming words on my toddler's tongue. I never called my Aunt Fannie Mae *Mother*. And my Grandma Matilda was just that—my grandma.

Mother.

I have a mother now.

That word keeps me company all through the night.

Detroit, Michigan
1947

I shall allow no man to belittle
my soul by making me hate him.
—Booker T. Washington

Twenty-Two

A NEW YEAR HAS COME AND MOTHER SAYS IT'S
time to reflect on all God has done. While making New
Year's resolutions, we also count our blessings and retell
stories about the past year and the lessons we have learned
and what we can do to be better this year. Summer blessings were trips to Belle Isle, running outside to the ice cream
truck, and late nights sitting on the porch with Mother.
Summer blessings were saving money to buy fabric and
practice, practice, practice with the patterns that Mrs. Collins gave me to work on till fall.

And in the fall, blessings came in the soft and comfort-
ing breeze, walks through crisp leaves that crunched and

crackled under my boots, hot apple cider, and a feast for Thanksgiving after volunteering to feed people without food and family.

Winter blessings were heavy and thick like Mother's pot of homemade stew, like the knitted hat and scarf she makes me wear when it snows, when the cold pierces my skin, freezes my bones.

Blessings, blessings, so many blessings: This past year, Father had more customers than ever before. And we've signed up more women for the Housewives' League. I became better at memorizing scriptures, talking into a microphone, and standing before the congregation to lead prayer.

Blessings, blessings, so many blessings: How Shirley and Jimmie and Juanita are getting bigger and smarter, how they are my little chocolate drops—each one of them. How Suesetta is still my best friend, my best everything.

Blessings, blessings. So many I lose count.

Twenty-Three

PHYLLIS HAS A NEW BEST FRIEND, LORETTA. This means that we walk separate ways now when going home and that we don't swap candy at lunch or pass notes in class or help each other with our homework. I miss Phyllis. Miss her strut and the way she shakes, shakes, shakes next to me when we dance, sweating out her hair and complaining that her press and curl is ruined. I miss her laugh, the way it starts like a pianist's solo, soft and low and then crescendoing and filling the room.

Without Phyllis's records, Suesetta and I have run out of new music to dance to. Suesetta's mom doesn't have any records that we like, and Mother and Father mostly only listen to Mahalia Jackson. So today Suesetta and I are going to Joe's Record Shop on Hastings.

Hastings Street is the spine of Paradise Valley. Walking down Hastings makes me think about what my life will be like when I'm grown and old enough to come here without telling Mother or Father where I'm going or what time I'm coming home. Makes me think about when I'll be in college wearing lipstick and high heels, and driving my own car. I'll meet up with friends at one of these restaurants, have supper, then go across the street to dance at one of the ballrooms and listen to Sarah Vaughan or Cab Calloway.

Joe's Records is packed with customers. The walls are covered with posters of all the greats. "Okay, how many do we want to buy?" I ask Suesetta.

"*We* can't buy anything, Betty. I don't have any money. I thought we were just looking."

"Just looking? We're buying at least one Billy Eckstine record," I say. "I have money. I have my savings. I brought fifty cents for our records and candy. Here, take half."

There is joy and sadness in Suesetta's eyes when I say this. "I'll pay you back," she says.

"You can't pay people back for a gift," I tell her. I pick up a record. "What about this one?"

"It's Billie Holiday," she tells me, like I don't already see that.

"I know. I like her, too, and it's on sale."

Suesetta holds on to it as we walk through the store, searching for a Billy Eckstine record. I'm looking through the third section of the vinyl records on sale when Suesetta yells, "Found one!" She holds up the record and passes it to me. "Not on sale, though," she says.

"It's okay. I think I have enough." I check my coin purse to make sure before going up to the counter. We won't be able to get candy for a few days, but that's okay.

On the way home, all Suesetta can talk about is the boycott we will be having next month at one of the local grocery stores that still refuses to hire coloreds. Suesetta and I helped design the flyers that we will hand out to people who are entering the store. "I'm nervous, aren't you?" Suesetta asks me.

"Not at all. What are you nervous about?"

"Well, this is different from going door-to-door telling

people what stores they shouldn't support. This time we'll actually be at the store we're boycotting, asking people not to buy there—*as* they are attempting to enter the store. I don't know, that just makes me nervous."

"When you feel nervous, remember what Mrs. Peck says: it's okay to be afraid if you know you're doing the right thing—just push right through your fears."

"Right," Suesetta says. "Just push through."

"I'm excited," I tell her. "We actually get to change people's minds right on the spot as they're walking in. Can you imagine how confused the owner will be when all his Negro customers see us standing there, take one of our coupons, and walk the other way? Leaving to shop with their hard-earned money across the street, where they are respected?"

The thought puts a smile on Suesetta's face.

"Hurt them in their pocket," I say. Mother always says that phrase. She also says that sometimes change comes reluctantly and out of dire necessity, not from true goodwill or pure values. "Some people have to feel the pain in order to believe in the medicine. And that's just fine. They are going to hurt in their pockets when they have more mer-chandise coming in than they have going out. And *that's* when they'll realize they should start listening to their Negro customers," I say, like Mother taught me.

As we walk, snowflakes twirl like ballerinas and land on the ground, creating a soft pillow to walk on. We turn onto our block and see an ambulance in front of Suesetta's house. I start walking faster, Suesetta runs. Kay is on the front porch with her brother, who is crying. Bernice is stand-ing next to them. Mother is consoling Aunt Nina, saying over and over, "He's going to be all right. Just trust the Lord, dearheart. Trust the Lord."

Once I am closer to the ambulance, I see Uncle Clyde on a stretcher. Suesetta goes up to her mom. "What hap-pened? What's wrong?"

"I don't know. He had a fever all day. Thought it was the flu, but then he started coughing uncontrollably, and he just—he just collapsed in the living room."

The ambulance drives off. Mother tells Aunt Nina and Suesetta's mother to get in her car so she can take them to the hospital. They leave us standing under the snow-filled sky. "I can stay with you tonight," I say to Suesetta and Kay. Neither of them answers.

Suesetta is a statue, stuck in fear or shock. I take her hand, walk her into her house. Kay follows us, closes the door, and locks it. The house is quiet. Kay puts Allen and Bernice to bed. Once the kids are asleep, the three of us sit in Suesetta's room, me on the floor, Kay across from me, Suesetta on her bed. I can't take the silence. I think maybe some music will help lift our spirits. I go to put on Billy Eckstine, but decide to play Billie Holiday instead. Let her sing our blues.

Twenty-Four

OVER THE NEXT THREE WEEKS, I HARDLY SPEND
any time with Suesetta. Uncle Clyde has TB—tuberculosis—
and has been quarantined at the hospital. Suesetta has been
quiet at school, and on the weekends she doesn't do much.
But today, I'm grateful she's decided to come to the boycott
of Jerry's Market.

Before we leave, I ask her how Uncle Clyde is doing.

"Not so good," she says. "My mom is heartbroken. He's
her only brother." Suesetta stops talking. Like she knows
the more she talks about it, the more likely she is to cry.

Mother comes out of her bedroom and down the stairs
ready to drive us to the market. When we get there, Mrs.

Ruth and Mrs. Peck are already putting flyers in people's hands. Mrs. Ruth is talking to a customer who's entering the store. "Did you know that this grocer refuses to hire Negro workers? Don't spend money where your people aren't respected and can't earn a living," she says. She holds out a flyer. The woman takes it, looks it over, and walks back to her car.

The next person walks right past Mrs. Ruth, not making eye contact and not letting her get one word out, but Mrs. Ruth just keeps right at it. "Excuse me, sir," she says to the next person. And she repeats her pitch.

We greet one another and join right in. We've been here for only five minutes when the manager of the store comes out and says, "You Negroes stop harassing my customers." He is a short, round man, and if he hadn't said *my customers*, I would have thought he was a customer himself, not the owner.

Mother says, "Sir, we are not harassing anyone. We are passing out flyers."

"If you don't get off my property, I'm calling the police to haul you out of here." He steps toward Mother. Yells at her so full of fury that spit flies out of his mouth as he enunciates every single word. This isn't a friendly *Sorry, ma'am, you can't pass those out* type of warning. This feels hostile, sounds like he's upset about so much more than just these flyers.

I've never seen anyone filled with so much hate. I've never seen anyone disrespect Mother. She turns to me and Suesetta, says, "Go wait in the car. And when you get in, look straight ahead, don't look out the windows. You understand?"

I don't want to leave her, but I know this is an order, not a suggestion, so I say, "Yes, ma'am." I don't look back as we walk and I don't look out the windows once we're in the car, but Suesetta can't help herself. We sit there waiting and waiting. "What's happening?" I ask.

"Mrs. Malloy is still talking to the owner . . . People are crowding around . . . Mrs. Ruth looks like she's yelling . . . Mrs. Peck is trying to calm her down," she tells me. Then, "They're coming, they're coming!" She turns around and looks straight forward.

When Mother gets in the car, she doesn't say a word about what just happened. She simply drives off, waving to

Mrs. Ruth and Mrs. Peck as they continue walking to Mrs. Peck's car. I can't take the silence. I ask, "Did you leave because he was going to call the police?"

"Betty, everything is fine."

"Is the Housewives' League in trouble?"

"Betty, everything is fine."

Suesetta says, "But what are we—"

"Girls, everything is fine."

We drive two blocks without talking. Then Mother says, "The good thing is, there were people who left and went to another store. We raised awareness today."

I think this is Mother's way of finding the good and praising it. But to me, having anyone standing so close to you that his breath slaps your face is not a blessing to count.

When we get home, Suesetta asks if she can come over. We go to the kitchen and eat sliced apples and peanut butter for an afternoon snack. I am so hungry, I finish my apples first. Suesetta eats so slow, I think that by the time she finishes, the sun will be setting and it'll be time for her to go home. While I wait for her to take her last bite, I look through the latest issue of *Ebony*. Mother gets the magazine every month and we look through it together. I start reading the article on Duke Ellington, how he performed at Carnegie Hall, how all of New York is in love with him. Makes me want to go to New York and boogaloo on a dance floor. I know Mother would never allow that, but I dream about it, still.

I flip through the magazine and stop at an advertisement for Nadinola Bleaching Cream. The caption reads, "The Nicest Things Happen to Girls with Light, Bright Complexions!" There's a woman with tan skin smiling and talking on the phone. Her hair is full of waves and pulled in an updo and she is wearing a strapless gown. Suesetta looks at the magazine ad and asks me, "Betty, you ever think about bleaching your skin?"

"What are you trying to say?" I ask.

Nothing but *crunch, crunch, swallow* from Suesetta.

"You think I need—"

"I'm just asking if you've ever thought about it," Suesetta says.

Suesetta licks a dollop of peanut butter and waits for my answer.

"Well . . . no," I say.

"Never?"

I think about it. "No, I—I like my complexion," I tell her.

She looks at me with surprise in her eyes. Like she can't believe I like my skin just the way it is. I throw her a look. "So what are you trying to say?" I ask.

"No, no," Suesetta says. "Not saying anything bad. I'm just surprised because it seems like everyone wants to change *something* about their looks," she tells me. "You know? Brunettes want to be blondes. People with curly hair want it to be straight. People with brown skin want—"

"Not me," I say. And right then, all the times my Aunt Fannie Mae told me I was her little chocolate drop come to mind and I think about Mother and how she always asks me if I know how beautiful I am. I tell Suesetta, "I think God made us the way He wanted us to be. I think maybe we make Him sad when we don't like how He made us, like we're telling Him that what He created was wrong."

Twenty-Five

TWICE A MONTH WE GO BACK TO JERRY'S
Market to pass out flyers. Every time we go, the owner forbids us to return. And even though some people take our flyers and coupons, many people walk right on in past us. We've been at it for four months and the store still refuses to hire Negroes.

Today was no different.

I am hoping the owner changes his mind by the end of summer. It's June, so we've got four more tries.

I'm sitting on my porch with Kay, trying not to think about Jerry's Market, or the fact that Uncle Clyde is still sick, or that Phyllis still isn't friends with Suesetta and me anymore. The ice cream truck just passed and we both bought an ice cream cone. Suesetta said she didn't want any even after I offered to buy it for her. She's in the house with Bernice.

I lick my butter pecan scoops and say to Kay, "Remember when I asked you if you thought being adopted was a big deal?"

"Yeah," Kay says.

"Well, I've been thinking about something else that's a big deal that adults don't talk about."

"What?"

"Stuff like what happened today—nothing seems to be changing and no one is talking about it."

"What do you want people to say?"

"I don't know, but colored people should say something," I tell her. I'm not sure what I want people to say, but I know I don't want to keep acting like I'm not upset. "When all those famous people come to our church talking about how we need to take a stand, how we need to fight, they never talk about what to do when we lose the fight. We lost today. We've been losing. My mother just says to find the good and praise it, but that doesn't fix anything."

"Maybe there is no fixing it," Kay says. "Maybe it's like Pastor Dames says—we have to keep sowing love and goodness in the world even when the world hates us. Remember? We reap what we sow."

"Yeah, but why do they hate us? How long are we supposed to wait for our harvest?"

Kay has no answer for this.

Maybe no one does.

❧

After Kay leaves, I go inside and get right to sewing. I begin working on the skirt Mrs. Collins taught us how to make. Besides listening to music and dancing, sewing is the thing that relaxes me. My mind empties and my thoughts settle. Out of all the things I have to do in life—chores, church, work, volunteering, school—sewing is where *I* make the decisions. I enjoy building new creations. And even when I mess up, I just pull out the thread and start all over again until I get it right.

I don't notice how long I've been working until Mother says, "You're still at it, huh? I think you need to take a break."

When she says this, I realize that I am hungry, and so I stop and we eat together. "I have a few errands to run before the sun goes down. Would you like to come with me?" Mother asks.

"Sure," I say.

We drive to all the places Mother needs to go—the cleaners, the post office. At every stop, I pay close attention to the women wearing skirts. I watch how different skirts flow, the way they hang depending on a woman's height, her shape, the design of the dress. I study the ease of the fabric, how some skirts swing like a bell and some lie stiff and barely move at all.

On our way back home, I tell Mother how I think Suesetta really wanted ice cream but couldn't afford it. I tell her, "I pray for Suesetta's family every night."

"That's good, Betty."

"But you always say faith without works is dead, so I would like to do something nice for them."

"What do you have in mind?" Mother asks.

I think about it. At first I think we could get them ice cream, but then I think that maybe they need more than a treat. "What about a basket of groceries?" I ask. I've helped Mother deliver her special baskets before. She has a closet full of wicker baskets of all sizes that she fills up with groceries for people in need. Mother has a heart as big as the sky.

She turns down a street that takes us to the grocer she likes to go to. We buy some of the things I know Suesetta and her family love and when we get home, we arrange everything in the basket. We make it look like more than just fruits and vegetables, breads and cheeses—we make it look special. We take the basket to Suesetta's house. The whole family becomes a chorus of *thank-you*s.

Later, when I get in bed and say my prayers, I think about Jerry's Market and how hard it is for the Housewives' League to change his mind. I think how there really are just some things that have nothing good, nothing worthy of praise. But still, there are other blessings.

I fall asleep counting them:

My hands that make it possible to carry a basket of groceries to a family in need.

The front porch to sit on and talk with a friend.

Records that spin and spin, filling up my room with joy again.

Twenty-Six

CHURCH DOESN'T FEEL THE SAME TODAY.

Pastor Dames announces that Deacon Willis passed away last night. A fog of grief hangs over the sanctuary. He'd been diagnosed with tuberculosis and was sick a lot less time than Uncle Clyde was. I know Suesetta is thinking, *If Deacon Willis wasn't as sick as Uncle Clyde, will Uncle Clyde die, too?* I take her hand, at first just to hold it during prayer, but then I keep holding it through the choir's first and second songs, the sermon, and the special prayer Pastor Dames says at the end of service for all the sick members of the church. Pastor Dames ends his prayer, saying, "Lord, we pray for all families with a loved one who is suffering."

When he says this, Suesetta squeezes my hand and we both say amen at the same time, but now is no time for a pinkie swear, so we look at each other with a half smile.

After church I sit in the last pew with Shirley, Jimmie, and Juanita, keeping an eye on them while Ollie Mae talks with Mrs. Murphy. I ask Shirley, "How is everybody?"

"Fine," Shirley says.

Jimmie and Juanita are playing with the Bibles and hymnals, sliding them and rearranging them.

Shirley tells me, "Momma's birthday is coming up."

"What are you going to get her?" I ask. I know how birthdays are a big deal with Ollie Mae. She says birthdays are our own personal holiday.

"Papa said we're going to take her out for dinner, but I want to do something else, too."

"You should make her something," I tell Shirley. "You're so good at drawing. You could draw something and we could frame it."

"Yeah, and Jimmie and Juanita can help, too. They're pretty good at coloring, so maybe they can help with that."

I can tell Shirley's mind has gone on to thinking about

what she'll draw for Ollie Mae. "What are you going to give Momma?" she asks.

I don't say anything for a while. I shrug, tell Shirley, "I don't know. I'll think of something."

"You could draw something, too," Shirley says.

"I'm not good at drawing. Besides, you're doing that."

"You could make her a cake," Shirley says.

When Shirley says this, I get an idea. I won't make Ollie Mae a cake, but I will make her something special.

❧

The sky gets hotter and hotter with each passing day. July's sun beams down bright and lasts long into the evening. Today, I am adding the finishing touches to my blouse and skirt for Ollie Mae. She usually wears dresses, and I have no idea what she'll think of me making her something, giving her something. Seems like she can't take anything from me except my help watching Shirley, Juanita, and Jimmie. She doesn't even say a friendly *How are you?* or *Do you have any special plans for this week?* When I try to talk with her, she just complains, "Child, if I had a coin for every question you ask . . ."

When I finish with the garments, I wrap them in the leftover paper Mother bought last Christmas. It seems silly to give someone a gift in July that's wrapped in holiday paper, but it's all there is and I've spent my candy and records budget on the fabric, buttons, and zipper.

Father puts the gifts in the trunk of the car. As we walk inside the sanctuary, Mother tells me, "Now do it discreetly, okay? Call her over to the car and give your gifts to her in private."

"Yes, ma'am," I say.

All through church the only thing I can think about is giving my gift to Ollie Mae.

At the end of service, Pastor Dames reminds everyone that today we are having a family day barbecue out back. Once he dismisses us, the congregation goes outside, where a few of the deacons are flipping burgers and hot dogs on the grills. The women have set up long tables and laid out side dishes, desserts, and cold drinks. Some of the younger children are already playing with water balloons.

I ask Ollie Mae to walk to the car with me. "What's over there, child?" she asks.

"I have a surprise for you," I say.

"Shirley, keep an eye on your sisters," Ollie Mae says. She walks to the parking lot. I follow her, keys in hand, and open the trunk. I take the gifts out and hand them to Ollie Mae. "What is all of this?" she asks.

"It's for you. Open them."

Ollie Mae sighs, like she would rather I just tell her.

"Happy birthday!"

"But my birthday isn't for three more days."

"I know, but I won't see you so I thought I'd give them to you today."

"I . . . You didn't have to—I can't accept this."

"But it's your birthday gift," I tell her.

Ollie Mae hands the boxes back to me. "You didn't have to give me anything." She starts to walk away. "I don't want you spending money on me, Betty Dean."

"But I—I made this. Can you open it?" I call out to her, "I just wanted to show you how much I appreciate the sewing machine. Just wanted you to know that I still have it and use it almost every day, and how much I practice, just like you."

I don't think Ollie Mae even hears me.

I stand in the parking lot holding the boxes, not able to move or speak or do anything. I don't know how much time passes before Kay is standing next to me. I don't realize that she's holding my hand until she says my name. "Betty? Betty, not here. Don't cry. Not here," Kay says. I put the gift back in the trunk. "Come with me. Let's walk," Kay says. She leads the way down the block, past the candy store, the bakery, the diner, to the park on the corner. We don't talk on our way. When we get to the park, we sit on swings and barely muster a sway. "What happened?" she asks.

I tell her about Ollie Mae. Tell her how mean she is, how she gave back my gift. A gift that I had made with my own hands, just for her. I tell Kay, "What's the point of doing unto others as you want them to do for you if this is what you get in return?"

Kay doesn't answer.

"And Pastor Dames can keep all those scriptures about sowing and reaping, because no matter how much good I try to do for Ollie Mae, nothing changes in our relationship. I just want her to love me. And even the Housewives' League keeps trying to do good, but things aren't *really* changing there, either. There are still stores that refuse to hire Negroes, still places where we go and get treated like we're nothing." My feet drag along in the dirt, then I push myself just a little and swing back and forth.

Kay lets me sit in my sadness for a moment longer before asking, "Betty, have you ever planted anything?"

"No."

"Well, *I* have. It's hard work," Kay says. "My family had a farm down South. I helped my mom with the garden. Before we could even plant, we'd have to get rid of the rocks, do a lot of digging, and do what my mom calls 'breaking the earth.'" Kay is swinging now. Back and forth, back and forth. She says, "When I first started helping in the garden, I was like you."

"What do you mean?" I ask.

"I was impatient and I didn't understand how seeds and harvesttime work. I thought as soon as I planted the seeds, I'd see growth the next day. But sometimes we wouldn't see any sign of growth for ten days, or seventy, or even three years."

"Three years?"

"The apple tree my dad planted took forever to have fruit. I'd walk past it every day for three years, just waiting."

"I'd be miserable if I had to wait that long. Didn't you get frustrated?"

"Well, there was always work to do somewhere else on the farm. Depending on the time of the year, something is always being planted, or taking root, or being watered, or sprouting. And then there was the prepping for winter and recovering from seasons when there was a bad crop—so, yes, we got frustrated a lot. Sometimes my mom would cry, she'd be so devastated. We had done the best we could and, all because of a drought or too much rain, we'd lose everything," Kay says. "But just because you have a bad season doesn't mean you stop planting."

We swing, propelling ourselves into the sky. No words, just the squeaky swing set, the clinking chains. Kay says, "I think maybe that scripture is not only about the harvest, but the work it takes to get a harvest, and the patience it takes to wait."

Twenty-Seven

I AM SITTING ON THE PORCH WATCHING Suesetta and Kay, who are pacing back and forth, looking down the street. Uncle Clyde is coming home from the hospital today. Aunt Nina left with Father to pick him up. Every time a car turns down our street we all hold our breath, but then when it doesn't slow down and stop, we keep talking.

"You think he'll be tired when he gets here? Maybe he won't want the lunch we made for him," Suesetta says.

"He'll probably be hungry for a good, home-cooked meal," Kay says.

I hear a car coming and see it's Father driving onto the

street. I stand up, walk down the steps. We all crowd at the curb, waiting for him to pull the car up to the house. "Step back, step back," Kay says. She is smiling and crying all at once.

Father parks the car, gets out, and helps Uncle Clyde up the steps. Uncle Clyde is thinner and moving slower, but when he sees us, he smiles the same smile. And his hello is all his—the way he sings it, holding on to the *o*. Kay gives him the first hug, then Suesetta, then the little ones come running out of the house, joy all over everybody's faces. I feel like I'm spying on something sacred, something not meant for people outside of their family to see, but then Aunt Nina calls over to me, says, "Go get your mother. Come on over and join us for lunch." And when we sit around the big table thanking God for this day, this moment, Aunt Nina prays, "And God, we especially thank you for the Malloys and Miss Betty. For without them being our extended family and being so kind and generous, we don't know what we would have done." In unison, everyone says, "Amen."

We eat and laugh and fill Uncle Clyde in on all that he

missed, but he can only take in so much. Soon, he is tired and we say our goodbyes so he can get settled and rest.

🐛

Later, before the sun goes down, I take out my notebook and write a letter to Ollie Mae. I fold it into an envelope and make my way to her house, the gifts tucked under my arm. When I get to the house, I don't knock or wait around to be seen. I put the boxes on the doorstep with the note and leave.

I think about what Kay said, think: *this is me watering the soil, this is me waiting for the harvest.*

Twenty-Eight

THE NEXT DAY THE DOORBELL RINGS, AND when I go to answer, I peep through the hole and I see a white lady standing at the door. She is fidgeting with her clothes, her hair, her purse. I call to Mother. She opens the door.

"Mrs. Malloy?"

"Yes."

She stammers, "Hi, I, uh, I am Rebecca Olsen. My husband and I just opened a little bakery not too far from here. I've heard about your Housewives' League campaign, and I, uh, I'm hoping we can talk about ways I can support your efforts."

Never could I have imagined that a white person would show up on our doorstep and offer to join our campaign.

"Well, nice to meet you. Why don't you come on in," Mother says.

They sit in the living room. I get a serving tray with a pitcher of lemonade and two glasses and serve them.

Before Mother even asks me, I go to my room. I know this is a conversation for adults. I leave the door cracked open just a bit. I sit on the floor right next to the door so I can hear what they're talking about.

Mother says, "What can I do for you, Mrs. Olsen?"

"I'll get right to it, if you, uh, if you don't mind."

"Don't mind at all, dear."

The two of them talk for an hour and by the time they finish, Mrs. Olsen has promised to accept Negroes to apply for work at her bakery. "And I'll see to it that they are not just hired, but that they are treated equally," she says. "Our store is one you will be able to guarantee on the list of places you encourage your community to patronize." Just as Mrs. Olsen leaves, she says, "Mrs. Malloy, please consider me a friend."

I look through the crack from my bedroom door and see Mrs. Olsen and Mother shaking hands.

As soon as Mrs. Olsen leaves, Mother sits down and telephones Mrs. Peck. "Fannie, you are not going to believe this," she says. "God has opened a door we didn't even knock on."

❧

The next time we're in church, Pastor Dames asks, "Are there any testimonies in the house?"

Mrs. Peck calls Mother up to tell their story. The church is full of whispers and praises, and more and more people stand in line at the microphone to tell of God's goodness. Aunt Nina and Uncle Clyde are next, and both of them are overflowing with tears and gratitude. They can't even finish talking they are so moved.

And then, Ollie Mae walks to the microphone. "Church, I'll be brief," she says. "I am thanking God today for His grace and mercy." She goes on to talk about the goodness of the Lord. I look at her and it takes a moment for me to really believe what I am seeing, because at first it looks like she is wearing something I've seen before, but under that familiar blazer is the blouse I made her. She's wearing the skirt, too.

And they're both a perfect fit.

Detroit, Michigan
1948

Freedom
Is a strong seed.
—Langston Hughes

Twenty-Nine

COUNTING BLESSINGS:

I could count all the times I had a snowball fight with Suesetta and Bernice, all the times I tried to sew a dress and failed, then tried again and made it just right. I could count how many laughs Shirley and I shared, how many times I told Jimmie and Juanita that I love them more than any of my favorite possessions. I could count the hugs from Mrs. Collins, the smiles from Mrs. Peck. I could count every nod from a stranger who passes by. I could count each rising and setting of the sun, every glistening star in the night sky.

But that would be too many numbers and I might not ever fall asleep.

Thirty

SCHOOL JUST LET OUT FOR SUMMER AND THE
next time I enter a school building, it will be Northern
High. Shirley keeps asking me if I'm scared to go to high
school, and how does it feel to be so grown up, and what
am I excited about the most. I don't really have all the answers, except to say that I can't wait to join the Delta Sigma
Theta Sorority. As a high school student, I can join the Delsprites. It's by invitation only and today, my invitation came.

Being a Delsprite means red will be one of my favorite
colors, second to purple. I'll get to go to debutante balls
and dinner parties, but the best part will be volunteering
for local organizations that work with children. I think I'd

be good at that since Mother is always saying that I have lots of compassion. Plus, I'm a good big sister, so it's probably the same kind of thing.

Suesetta hasn't received her invitation yet, but I'm sure it's coming. We're walking home from the park plotting out what we want our first year of high school to be like. The June sky dripped its sunshine on us all day. All afternoon we feasted on Popsicles to keep cool. Now our tongues are rainbows.

The day faded and now the sun is sleeping and the stars are awake and dancing above us. We are about three blocks away from my house when a boy runs down the street, yelling, "The police out here are killing people! The police out here are killing people!" The boy runs right past us, yelling the whole way. Porches fill up with curious neighbors who've come outside to see what all the commotion is about. They tell us, "You all hurry and get home, you hear? Hurry and get home." A man comes outside and walks us.

We walk faster than I've ever walked, and when I get to my house, Mother insists that Father turn the radio off and I get ready for bed.

It isn't until the next morning that I learn what happened. Father and I are sitting at the dining room table listening to the radio. A man's voice just announced that Leon Mosley, a fifteen-year-old Negro boy, was shot in the back by the police. He died. "Police say he was joyriding in a stolen car after attending a dance," the voice says so matter-of-factly, so empty of any feeling.

Mother comes into the kitchen and before she says *Good morning* or asks *How did you sleep?* she starts fussing at Father. "Lorenzo, now, this is no way to start the morning. Please turn that off."

Father gets up and turns the knob slow enough that we hear the voice say there are conflicting eyewitness stories about what happened before the officer shot Leon— some say they beat the boy and he broke free, was running away, and then they shot him. Others don't mention a beating, just say he was shot. But all eleven witnesses say he was shot in the back, which means he didn't pose a threat to anyone.

They didn't have to shoot him, kill him dead. Did they?

Now that the radio is off, the dining room is silent like

a moonless sky. I can't eat my breakfast. I feel sick and all I want to do is go back to yesterday, when it was a nice June day and the sun was melting my Popsicle and I was dreaming of being a Delsprite and walking and talking in the park with Suesetta.

Just as I am thinking this, there's a knock on our door. Kay and Suesetta are standing there, all dressed up in their finest. Kay says, "There's going to be a march this afternoon. We stopped by to see if you want to come."

Seeing them on my doorstep reminds me of Phyllis. We haven't talked in a while, except for a casual hello at church. But looking at Suesetta and Kay right now makes me remember everything Phyllis said about how silly we were to think that passing out flyers would change things. "Um, I'm going to stay home today."

They both look surprised, but they don't push me to change my mind.

I close the door and join Mother in the kitchen as she starts our Saturday-morning cleaning. She hands me a bottle of bleach. "Pour a little of this into that water and add some soap."

I take the bleach, pour a capful into the bucket of water so I can mop.

"Not too much now," Mother says. "Too much and we'll get to coughing and our eyes will be stinging."

I mop the floor, she washes dishes, and we go about our cleaning like this is a regular day. But there is nothing normal about today. The whole time we clean, I whisper a prayer for the family of the fifteen-year-old boy with a bullet in his back lying somewhere in a morgue.

Leon Mosley. He is one year older than me and gone. I think of all the colored people's lives that were here one minute, gone the next. The ones I saw hanging from trees when I was just a little girl.

My eyes are watering. I look at Mother, see tears welling in her eyes, too. And the burning has nothing to do with the bleach.

Thirty-One

IT'S HARD TO COUNT BLESSINGS THIS WEEK.

Should I be thankful for the people marching, thankful that they are using their voices to speak up, speak out? Should I be thankful for the lawyers who are working for half their pay to make sure there is justice for the boy whose heart is no longer beating? Should I be thankful that it wasn't someone I knew?

It is hard to count blessings this week.

So instead, I just pray. I pray for peace, for Leon Mosley's family. I pray that one day I won't ever have to pray these kinds of prayers.

Thirty-Two

IT'S BEEN A WEEK SINCE LEON MOSLEY DIED.
Protesters have been marching every day. But today, the streets are clear and quiet. Today is the first day that things feel normal again. I am sitting in my room listening to the radio. A Billy Eckstine song comes on—an old one that I haven't heard in a long while. After the song ends, the DJ announces that Billy Eckstine is coming to Detroit next month for a special concert at one of the jazz supper clubs. The DJ plays another of his songs. I lie on my bed and daydream about the day I'll actually be able to go to one of his concerts. I think up ways I could maybe even get a glimpse of him while he's in town. If I stand outside the

backstage door after the concert, I might see him as he leaves. But I know Mother would never let me out that late, so I just turn the radio up and enjoy his singing from the airwaves.

Listening to this song makes me think of Phyllis.

I pick up the phone and call her. I don't really plan to do this, it just happens. On the first ring, I think maybe I should hang up. I don't know what to say but then, the phone rings a second time and she picks up.

"Hello?"

"Hi, Phyllis. It's Betty."

She hesitates. "Oh, hi, Betty."

Both of us sit on the phone waiting for the other to speak. I'm the one who called, so I know it needs to be me. What do you say to someone you haven't spoken to in so long? "I, uh, I was just calling to say hello," I tell her.

"Oh."

I clear my throat. Try to think of something to say. "Have you heard about Leon Mosley?" I ask.

"So sad," she says. "It's just awful."

"I heard on the radio that there's a way to donate and

send money to the family to help pay for his funeral," I tell her.

"Really?" she says.

There is silence again and then I say, "I was thinking about donating. Maybe . . . Do you think . . . we could put our money together and donate something?"

Phyllis doesn't respond right away.

"And I can ask Suesetta, too," I tell her.

Then Phyllis says, "Maybe we can ask Bethel to take up a special offering. His family doesn't go to our church, but we could still help out."

And just like that we are talking again and making plans to ask Pastor Dames before church next Sunday if Bethel can help the Mosley family.

I don't know if this means we'll ever dance together again or look through magazines and plan trips to Harlem, but it feels good knowing that we can come together when it matters most.

As soon as I hang up the phone, I call Suesetta. It is not time to go to bed yet, but already I know the blessing I will be counting tonight.

Thirty-Three

THE NAACP IS HAVING A SPECIAL CEREMONY to honor local Negro leaders in Detroit. Suesetta and I are volunteering to be greeters. Mother tells me there will be many special guests and that the League chose us to be greeters because they can trust that we will be good hosts.

The banquet hall is a paradise of a place. On the first floor, all of the chairs are covered in white cloth and tied across the back with flowing pine-green ribbon that has silver piped along the edges. The white flowers in the centerpieces rise high and perfume the room. They are surrounded by small white candles that sit on the tables, making shadows and shapes on the tablecloths. Tall, heavy white drapes cover the backdrop of the entire stage, which is ready with microphones, three music stands, and a black baby-grand piano. It feels strange to be in the center of all this beauty when so much ugliness has been happening.

"You two will stand at the door and greet everyone. Give each person a program," Mrs. Peck says.

Mother adds, "And when the program begins, you can go up to the balcony and watch the entertainment and speeches from there."

Suesetta and I take our posts. As guests arrive, we say hello and hand out the programs that are printed on ivory linen paper. I take in all the dresses glittering with sequins, the bow ties and matching handkerchiefs. Even though everyone is all dressed up and smiling, there is a heaviness in the room.

Pastor Dames walks onto the stage, and Suesetta and I go upstairs to the balcony. Up there, we have the perfect view of the whole banquet. The silverware sparkles under the glow of the candles and the servers begin bringing out the first course.

Pastor Dames opens the evening with a welcome that

sounds more like a sermon. "Good evening, friends," he says. "Difficult days are upon us."

Even though this isn't church, there are a few people who say amen, and heads are nodding in agreement.

Pastor Dames says, "I know that some of us are growing weary. But let me remind you that even in our darkest days there is much for which to be thankful. Let me remind you that with every great advancement this country has made, there has always been opposition for the Negro. Slavery, the Emancipation Proclamation, Reconstruction, Jim Crow, and yet we are still here." Pastor Dames pauses and then says, "Now, they asked me to do the welcome and the introduction. So let me first welcome you to the struggle. Let me invite you to continue the work. We must not back down, we must not give up. Let us keep pressing to witness that joy in the morning." Then he says, "Now, for all you young people in the room, let me tell you that when your time comes to pick up where us old folks leave off, you will have a road map to follow."

I look around the room at all these men and women

and think about each of us being someone's seed, someone's prayer, someone's hope.

Pastor Dames continues, "Now, for the welcome you're waiting for—ladies and gentlemen, without further ado, I introduce to you our musical guests for the evening, Billy Eckstine and Miss Sarah Vaughan!"

The banquet room erupts in cheers.

Suesetta and I are the loudest. Mother and Mrs. Peck look up at us, smiling. The music starts playing and when Sarah Vaughan and Billy Eckstine walk onto the stage, we scream even louder. I can't believe I'm actually looking at Sarah Vaughan and Billy Eckstine in the flesh. Right here, in front of me. Hearing him is better than any record I've ever heard, better than ice cream all day on your birthday.

They sing a duet and then each of them sings two songs. After Billy Eckstine finishes his last song, the applause continues like a mighty wind rustling through a forest of trees. And these trees have deep roots, so grounded that even though they bend, they don't break. So many of us bearing fruit, so many of us just planted.

Thirty-Four

I GET UP THE NEXT MORNING AND THE FIRST thing I realize is that last night, I fell right to sleep. No tossing and turning, no memories haunting me, no waking up in the middle of the night.

Before I get out of bed, I think maybe I should start my day the way I usually end it. In this moment while the sun is just waking and the house is still, I thank God for this brand-new day and begin to count my blessings:

The blessing of people coming together for a common cause.

The blessing of me being a part of them, and them a part of me.

The blessing of having a mother, a father.

The blessing of having my best friend forever, Suesetta, and each of my sisters and brothers and Arthur and even Ollie Mae.

The blessing of belonging to this struggle, this fight.

The blessing of giving love, of being loved.

Author's Note

"My most vivid memory of Betty is that she was first and foremost a woman who cherished her family. A wife and mother, she was extremely protective of her children. Mothers instinctively protect those they love, even more so in the face of danger. And, when you are the wife of a civil rights activist whose philosophy is perceived equally by blacks and whites as caustic, you become the shield that wards off the evil spears of hatred. You place yourself in harm's way."

—MYRLIE EVERS-WILLIAMS, ACTIVIST
AND WIFE OF CIVIL RIGHTS LEADER MEDGAR EVERS

My mother, Dr. Betty Shabazz, was a phenomenal woman. She was a nation builder. She is known to many as the wife of El Hajj Malik El Shabazz (Malcolm X), but so much of her legacy was rooted in her childhood experiences and bore fruit after my father's life ended. Her character is often commended by people who wonder how she was able to live under such fearful and challenging times as those of Jim Crow and the civil rights movement. I believe it was my mother's childhood that prepared her to become Malcolm X's wife, a mother of six daughters, an educator, and an advocate for girls and women. Her willingness to forgive, her passion for family, her love of sisterhood, and her dedication to standing up against injustice were cultivated in her early years. Once she married my father, she also married the struggle for freedom.

My mother witnessed the martyrdom of her husband on February 21, 1965. I was at the Audubon Ballroom with her and my elder sisters, Attallah and Qubilah, when my father was to deliver an address on his new federation, the Organization of Afro-American Unity. At the time, Mom was pregnant with my twin sisters, Malikah and Malaak. Gamilah, who was just a few months old, was at home with the Wallaces, who are family to Ossie Davis and Ruby Dee. Ossie Davis and his wife, Ruby Dee, were famous

African American television, film, and Broadway actors; playwrights; poets; authors; and civil rights activists. They were trusted and loyal friends to my parents. We were staying with the Wallaces because our own house had just been firebombed a week prior. Someone had thrown an explosive into the nursery where my sisters and I slept.

I have no clear recollection of that day at the Audubon Ballroom because I was not quite three years old. I am told that our mother literally shielded my sisters and me from the gunfire with her body before attempting to save her husband's life with mouth-to-mouth resuscitation.

In a matter of days, my mother's life changed forever. She was left alone—widowed, a single parent of four babies and pregnant with my youngest sisters, the twins. She was the wife of a man who challenged a system that was historically unjust to its own citizens, and so she was harassed by the Nation of Islam, the Federal Bureau of Investigation, and the Central Intelligence Agency.

I am grateful to Ruby Dee, Juanita Poitier, Nina Simone, and several other women in the arts who emotionally supported my mother during that time. I am further grateful to Gloria Steinem and Congresswoman Bella Abzug, who sold her home to Betty for a considerably lowered rate. Each of these women understood that it was her duty as a woman and a human being to help Betty however they could, considering all that Malcolm X contributed to the human race.

My mother persevered through this adversity because she possessed faith in God, respect for self, an awareness of history, and a perspective that never permitted her to say, "No, I can't accomplish this." As a child and as an adult, my mother refused to live her life as a victim or in despair. And as a result, she soared, all the while giving of herself to others. She often said to me, "Ilyasah, just as one must drink water, one must give back."

My mother was born Betty Dean Sanders in Pinehurst, Georgia. She eventually moved to Detroit, Michigan, where she attended middle school and high school. There she joined the marching band and played the drums. She also joined the Delta Sigma Theta Sprites. She was an excellent student and very hardworking. She was a member of the Bethel African Methodist Episcopal Church (AME), and worked at her father's shoe repair store. After high school, she attended the Tuskegee Normal and Industrial Institute in Alabama (the alma mater of her parents, Lorenzo and Helen Malloy). Returning to the South was challenging for my mother because of the oppressive Jim Crow laws. She refused to accept the mistreatment directed at African Americans and women. Her college counselor helped Betty to enroll in a Tuskegee program affiliate in the North. Young Betty courageously uprooted herself at the age of eighteen and relocated again, to Brooklyn, New York, where a relative from her father's side of the family lived. She attended Brooklyn State Hospital School of Nursing.

While pursuing her nursing-school studies, my mother was invited by a friend to attend a Nation of Islam meeting. There she heard a young, dynamic speaker named Malcolm X. After the speech, they discussed the racism she encountered in Alabama, and she began to understand its causes, pervasiveness, and effects. Soon, she would be attending *all* of my father's lectures.

Shortly after, Mom graduated from nursing school. Dad called her from a telephone booth and proposed to her. They were married within one week. Their relationship was a true example of partnership, undying love, devotion, and mutual respect.

Most of what I learned about my father and his teachings was communicated through my mother and her actions. She was determined to serve as an educator and role model, and to raise us six girls on her own. We attended private schools, summer camp in Vermont with Quaker and Native American values, music lessons, dance lessons, and tutorials in Islam and the history of the African Diaspora. My mother made sure that my sisters and I had a culturally rich and diverse education, and she made sure to continue her advocacy work. When we moved to Westchester County, my mother founded the Young Mothers Educational Development program. This initiative provided support for pregnant teens and made sure their educational aspirations would not be interrupted. Furthermore, she helped to open a day-care center so that once those teenage mothers delivered their babies, they had a safe place to leave their children while they continued pursuing their degrees.

Despite already having a nursing degree and a bachelor of arts in public health and education from Jersey City State College, my mother went on to earn a master of arts in public health education from Jersey City State College and a Ph.D. in education administration from the University of Massachusetts at Amherst. All alongside the challenge of raising six girls.

In 1976, Mom joined New York's Medgar Evers College as a professor. She taught health sciences, and then became head of public relations as well as serving as the school's cultural attaché. My mother took part in various United States delegations with Presidents Ford, Carter, and Clinton. She also participated in the Fourth World Conference on Women in Beijing, China, and continued to travel internationally for the cause of social justice. She was an outspoken advocate for human rights, women's rights, racial tolerance, and the goal of self-determination and self-reliance.

My mother passed away in 1997. Her *Janazah* was attended by such luminaries as Myrlie Evers-Williams,

Coretta Scott King, Maya Angelou, U.S. Representative Maxine Waters, and so many other distinguished leaders. Fittingly, her devotion to health issues was recognized when, in 1997, the Brooklyn Community Healthcare Network dedicated the Dr. Betty Shabazz Health Center in her honor. Medgar Evers College and the New York State legislature also honored Mom with the endowment of the Dr. Betty Shabazz Distinguished Chair in Social Justice.

My mother established the Malcolm X Medical Scholarship program for outstanding students attending Columbia University—where the recipient must commit to providing medical service to the underserved for at least one year. Subsequently, Columbia University established the Betty Shabazz Nursing Scholarship program. My mother was also relentless in convincing the United States government to honor her husband with a postage stamp featuring his image. She also formed a coalition of community, political, and educational leaders to establish the Malcolm X Memorial Center at the Audubon to honor her husband's legacy. After Mom passed away, we re-conceived it as the Malcolm X and Dr. Betty Shabazz Memorial and Educational Center.

It is my hope that by reading my mother's story, young people who may be feeling abandoned or neglected, fearful or hopeless, anxious or unsure, will find inspiration. Betty certainly experienced all of those feelings at one time or another. However, she rose to become a devoted wife, a selfless mother, a compassionate friend, a bold activist, and—most importantly—a caring human being who lived her life with integrity and grace. It is not falling that defines you, it's the process of what you determine to do each time you stand.

Thank you for reading her story. May God continue to bless you so we can have a society of peace, liberation, and pure freedom intended for every human being.

Detroit in the 1940s

The 1940s were years of tremendous growth for Detroit, but the decade also had great upheaval. An influx of African Americans moving to the city to work in the factories caused a housing crisis. Even though Jim Crow laws did not govern the North, racial tensions were still very real and there was resistance from many white people who refused to integrate or work with black people. Most black families lived on the city's east side in the neighborhoods of Paradise Valley and Black Bottom.

In Black Bottom, residents were often forced to squeeze into single-room houses, and there were many homes without cooking facilities or indoor plumbing. Paradise Valley was a hub for black-owned businesses, like grocery stores, bakeries, doctor's offices, and dry cleaners. Paradise Valley was most famous for its music and entertainment district. Local clubs hosted many nationally renowned performers, including Billy Ekstine, Sarah Vaughan, Ella Fitzgerald, Cab Calloway, Billie Holiday, and Duke Ellington.

Even though African Americans could go to public spaces where white people were, they often received poor service and endured many racist encounters. Tensions boiled over in the summer of 1943 and a race riot took place which lasted for over three days, killing thirty-four individuals and injuring hundreds.

Five years later, on June 4, 1948, Leon Mosley, a fifteen-year-old driving a stolen car, was beaten, shot in the back, and killed by officer Louis Melasi. This was not the first instance of police brutality in Detroit, and there was outrage from the community. Protesters demanded that the officer be arrested. Murder charges were filed against Officer Melasi. He went to trial on December 14, 1948, and was acquitted.

This was the backdrop to Betty's middle school years. Though she did not talk about any of this openly with her parents, the older she got, the better she understood Detroit's complicated history and her place in it.

Bethel AME Church

Bethel African Methodist Episcopal Church (AME), one of Detroit's largest and oldest congregations, had its beginnings in 1839 among a group of free black Methodists. Over the years and under the leadership of pastor William H. Peck, the church became a crucial part of the community. The church operated a credit union, offered food and clothing during the Great Depression, and established a curriculum that taught black history to its members.

Bethel AME was a popular speaking destination for black activists, politicians, and entertainers from around the nation. Regular guests included NAACP attorney Thurgood Marshall, who later became the first black justice on the U.S. Supreme Court. Paul Robeson, a human rights activist, actor, and singer, was also a frequent guest.

The black community—religious or not—depended on Bethel AME for everyday, practical needs. Every winter, the church hosted training for newly arrived residents from the South. One popular training gave tips to parents on how to dress their children during the blistering-cold months that Detroiters knew all too well, but that were foreign to people coming from the South.

Betty sang in the choir and attended Sunday school on a regular basis. Because Lorenzo and Helen Malloy were leaders in the church, Betty spent many weeknights there accompanying them for meetings and services. She enjoyed attending church and being involved in its programs. The church was a beacon of light and hope for the community.

Meet the Characters

Most of the main characters in this novel are based on real people. For the sake of simplicity, some characters are composites of several real people. In an attempt to provide a fuller picture of Detroit, some characters and situations are based on historical facts and are not literal accounts of Betty's life.

GRANDMA MATILDA AND AUNT FANNIE MAE

Grandma Matilda was Betty's paternal grandmother. Her son, Shelmon Sanders, was twenty-one at the time of Betty's birth. Matilda sent him to Philadelphia and changed his last name to Sandlin. It is true that Grandma Matilda saw a mark on Betty's neck and confronted Ollie Mae. When Ollie Mae could offer no explanation, Grandma Matilda took Betty, and Aunt Fannie Mae raised her. After Aunt Fannie Mae died, Betty moved to Detroit to live with her biological mother, Ollie Mae.

OLLIE MAE

Ollie Mae was sixteen years old and unmarried when she had Betty. After Ollie Mae moved to Detroit, she married Arthur Burke, who had two sons. Together, they had three daughters: Shirley, Jimmie, and Juanita. Though Ollie Mae was strict with all of her children, she and Betty had the most disagreements, and the most angst between them. As Betty grew older, she stayed in touch with her biological parents, Ollie Mae in Detroit and Shelmon in Philadelphia, and other members of her biological family—including her paternal siblings, Shelmon Sandlin II, the Reverend Stanley Sandlin, and John Sandlin, Esq.

LORENZO AND HELEN MALLOY

For the Malloys, faith came first. However, they were firm believers that after praying, one must get to work. They attended Bethel AME and were seen as extended family by many children at the church. Before taking Betty in, it was common for the Malloys to look after children from time to time to support distressed families. The couple believed in education, enterprise, and self-determination. Lorenzo Malloy prided himself on being a self-made businessman. He believed that if his business could thrive despite the Great Depression and World War II, any black person could find a way to be successful. While a student at the black Tuskegee Normal and Industrial Institute in Alabama, he met Booker T. Washington, the formerly enslaved young man who founded Tuskegee Normal. Lorenzo Malloy looked up to Washington and was inspired by his resilience and philosophy.

Helen Malloy was an active leader in the Housewives' League and also taught grammar school. When she wasn't working, she was at the church volunteering for various church programs, including vacation Bible school.

Helen raised Betty as her own daughter until Betty left for college. Though Mrs. Malloy encouraged Betty to be an active citizen by volunteering and canvassing on behalf of the Housewives' League, the NAACP, and the Delsprites, Mrs. Malloy did not openly talk about racism with her. She often encouraged Betty not to focus on the negative, but rather to "find the good and praise it." The one time Betty remembered her mother talking explicitly about race was just before she boarded the train to Alabama for college.

The Malloys were also an important part of Betty's adult life. Betty called her parents every Sunday, and Mrs. Malloy and Betty often wrote each other letters. Lorenzo Malloy died in 1960. Helen Malloy died in 1994 at the age of ninety-six.

SHIRLEY, JIMMIE, AND JUANITA

Betty loved her sisters deeply, and they adored her. The scenes in the book where the sisters interact with each other are based on family memories and the most recent interviews with the middle sister, Jimmie. After Betty moved in with the Malloys, she never returned to the home where her sisters lived. Betty stayed in touch with her sisters throughout her adult life.

SUESETTA, PHYLLIS, AND KAY

Betty's adult sister-friends called her loyal, forgiving, and extremely generous. She had a laugh that enveloped a room and was not quick to be judgmental or resentful. She was known as a friend who, no matter what she endured in her personal life, always brought joy to others. The friendships depicted in this novel were inspired by the recollections of some of her closest adult friends, as well as printed interviews.

One of Betty's childhood best friends in real life was named Suesetta. They loved baking cookies and talking about fashion. They enjoyed listening to Billy Eckstine, Billie Holiday, and Sarah Vaughan records on the weekends, and Suesetta loved the way Betty danced. Sometimes, when the girls were bored, they actually made prank calls, picking random numbers out of the phone book.

Phyllis is a fictional character representing the tension that was present in Detroit over the Housewives' League. Though the Housewives' League was nationally acclaimed, there were many black families who felt the group was out of touch with the real needs of the black community. There were families who could not afford to only buy from stores that sold products made by black people or employed black people. Oftentimes, those stores were more expensive. A major critique of the Housewives' League was that since very few of its members were blue-collar workers, the League was out of touch with what the majority of black people needed and wanted.

Kay, another fictional character, was inspired by oral histories recounting life for many African American families in Detroit in the 1940s. Because of the challenging conditions in Black Bottom, tuberculosis was common and many people had to be quarantined away from their homes, sometimes for months or years. These families suffered greatly due to the financial strain that came with caring for a loved one with an illness. Oftentimes, even after the patient was physically better, the emotional and mental toll it took on both the patient and the family never resolved.

MRS. PECK AND THE HOUSEWIVES' LEAGUE

Fannie B. Peck founded the Housewives' League of Detroit on June 10, 1930. She believed that it was women who spent the income of most households and that this gave them power. Where women spent money mattered, and she wanted to make sure black women were spending their money at black-owned businesses and in stores that hired black people and sold black products. These businesses included restaurants, grocery stores, florists, accounting and legal firms, funeral homes, car dealerships, and more.

The Housewives' League became a national movement, growing from just fifty to twelve thousand members in four years. The League also had an educational component for young women and held many contests, including annual scrapbook, essay, and queen contests. One cherished event was the annual Fannie B. Peck Day, a day designated to celebrate Mrs. Peck and her contributions to the organization.

Timeline

May 28, 1934

Betty is born to Ollie Mae and Shelmon Sanders in Pinehurst, Georgia.

1935

Betty's paternal grandmother, Matilda MacAfee Greene, takes Betty and gives her to Aunt Fannie Mae to raise.

1941

Aunt Fannie Mae dies. Betty moves to Detroit to live with Ollie Mae.

June 20, 1943

Race riots begin at Belle Isle and spread throughout Detroit.

September 2, 1945

World War II ends.

1945

Betty moves in with Lorenzo and Helen Malloy.

1948

Leon Mosley, a black fifteen-year-old, is beaten by white Detroit police officers for stealing a car. After beating him, they shoot him in the back, killing him. No officer is convicted.

1952

Betty graduates from Northern High School and attends one year of college at the Tuskegee Normal and Industrial Institute in Alabama.

1953

Betty leaves Alabama to study at the Brooklyn State Hospital School of Nursing in New York City.

1956

Betty meets Malcolm X, converts to the Nation of Islam, and changes her last name to "X" to represent her African ancestry and the loss of her name through the transatlantic slave trade.

January 14, 1958

Betty marries Malcolm X. The couple eventually has six daughters.

November 16, 1958

Attallah Shabazz is born.

December 25, 1960

Qubilah Shabazz is born.

July 22, 1962

Ilyasah Shabazz is born.

July 1, 1964

Gamilah-Lumumba Shabazz is born.

February 21, 1965

Malcolm X is assassinated while giving a speech at the Audubon Ballroom in New York City. Betty, pregnant with twins at the time, is in the audience with three of their daughters.

September 30, 1965

Twins Malikah and Malaak Shabazz are born.

1969

Betty completes a master's degree at Jersey City State College.

1975

Betty earns a Ph.D. in education administration from the University of Massachusetts.

1976

Betty begins working as a professor of health sciences at Brooklyn's Medgar Evers College.

June 23, 1997

Betty dies at Jacobi Medical Center in New York City after suffering severe burns in a house fire. She is buried on top of her husband, Malcolm X, at Ferncliff Cemetery in Hartsdale, New York.

Acknowledgments

I would like to express gratitude first and foremost to God the Almighty, and to the many people who aided me in the process of bringing this story to life. As always, I am grateful for the strength and support of my family, who share my commitment to imparting Betty's legacy to young people. My father for choosing my mother as his bride and keeper of the flame for future generations. My sisters, Attallah, Qubilah, Gamilah, Malikah, and Malaak, as well as my nephews and niece, Malcolm, Malik, and Bettih—eternal love and strength to each of you. Thank you, Attallah, for always being available to answer my questions about Daddy and about me. My mother's biological family members who shared many stories, especially Aunts Shirley and Jimmie, and Betty's dearest childhood friend, Suesetta MacCree, for her committed friendship eighty years later. To Princess Alia Al Hussein for your friendship and counsel.

Much gratitude to my agent, Jason Anthony of the Massie & McQuilkin Literary Agency, for bringing Renée Watson and me together. Thank you especially to Grace Elizabeth Kendall for her keen editorial eye, along with everyone at Farrar Straus Giroux and Macmillan Children's Publishing Group who helped transform this book from an idea to a reality. And to Renée Watson for helping to shape the story of my mother's childhood into this book.

A special thank-you to Marsha Battle Philpot for sharing her family's oral history with us. I would like to also acknowledge the Charles Wright Museum and significant citizens in the city of Detroit, including the Honorable JoAnn Watson, Jamon Jordan, and Charles Ezra Ferrell.